A Single Mistake

A Single Mistake

When justice fails, who pays the price?

Ashish Sharma

NU VOICE
PRESS

NU VOICE PRESS

First published by NU VOICE PRESS 2025
An imprint of Hubhawks Pvt. Ltd
www.nuvoicepress.com

ISBN: 978-81-993013-0-6

Printed at: Thomson Press India Ltd

Published by: Nu Voice Press

To my wife, Mrs Poonam Sharma, whose unwavering love and unconditional support granted me the privilege of devoting myself fully to my writing.

To my mother, Mrs Meenakshi Sharma, who has always been my greatest source of strength and inspiration, reminding me of the power and resilience of women.

It is because of these two remarkable women that my stories naturally find their way into the world of women.

DISCLAIMER

PROLOGUE

2015

The city suddenly found itself in the spotlight of state politics, basking in attention, when one of its own rose to the powerful position of home minister in the state cabinet. Overnight, the roads gleamed with fresh asphalt, hospitals expanded their facilities, schools received long, overdue grants, and a wave of development swept across the streets.

Yet, beneath coats of fresh paint and polished façades, the old rot still festered. Injustice wore newer clothes, and corruption walked down newer corridors. What changed was only the surface. The soul of the city remained the same. Crime was not uncommon here, just as in any other city. Despite the grand title of being the state's home minister's hometown, the crime rate remained disturbingly familiar. But no one knew that soon, a crime would occur. A crime that would shake not just the city, but the very foundation of its society.

A crime that would blur the lines between guilt and justice, silence and rebellion.

A *Bhasmasur*—a mythic demon from the Puranas who, once granted power, turned against his creator—was about to rise.

He would burn through social beliefs, leaving behind only ashes and questions.

I

July 2016

The city was in a state of shock. The lifeless body of a naked woman had been discovered in an abandoned school building. It appeared that someone, or more than one person, had assaulted her sexually, and she had died from heavy blood loss. A video was circulating on all social media platforms since that morning, displaying graphic images of the victim.

A kid spotted her body first. It was a Monday morning, and the incident had occurred perhaps the previous night. Her blood was scattered throughout the playground, and the bloody traces led up to Class Eight. This room was the crime scene, and a lot of blood was splattered there.

A flock of people gathered around the crime scene. People shot videos and clicked photos of the woman's body and the pooled blood on the ground. The news spread like wildfire in all the surrounding villages.

The police arrived late, and by then, people were roaming around as if it were a picnic spot. The investigating officer appealed to the people to leave the place, but no one paid any heed to his appeal. He had to call for more police forces from surrounding police stations. The increasing number of people forced the police to do a lathi charge; only then could they control the situation. The unrestricted movement at the crime scene destroyed many substantial pieces of evidence and traces.

Soon, these disturbing videos and photos became the point of discussion of the entire nation. Everyone was talking about them. It ran as breaking news on all news channels, and they named the victim "Sabala"—a powerful woman.

***

This incident shook state politics. The opposition was overly aggressive and vocal against the ruling party. In the Assembly, they raised their voices against the critical situation of law and order. The chief minister had to address the Assembly. He assured the community that not a single culprit would be able to escape. He declared that a special investigating team would be formed to handle the case. He tried to calm the public's anger and prevent the opposition from taking advantage of this incident by making this declaration. He called a meeting of all senior police officers and gave them clear-cut instructions to resolve this matter. The instructions were clear to the officers: either solve the case, or suppress the issue.

This incident was perplexing; it was difficult for the officials to solve the case. The pressure from the public and media was increasing day by day. The administration tried to stop the circulation of the photos and videos on social media and WhatsApp groups, but failed.

Protests, candle marches, and meetings against the government and police continued. One fine morning, the police officers called a press briefing and presented the culprit, one Chatar Singh, a forty-five-year-old van driver. He used to drive his van on one of the busiest routes in the city, carrying passengers on a sharing basis.

According to the police's story, he saw the victim alone at night at a bus stand and found her easy prey. He trapped her by offering a shared ride to her area and took her to the school, where he assaulted her at knifepoint. He kept her there as hostage for the night and repeated the barbaric act. Meanwhile, she started bleeding from her private organs, but he did not pay any heed to her pain.

Later that night, when the accused went to urinate, the victim got a chance to escape. She ran from the crime scene, but could only reach the hand pump situated in the playground. Due to heavy blood loss, she fainted there and died.

Police officers also showed her postmortem report. The postmortem report supported the police theory. The cause of death was excessive blood loss, and the time of death was between 2.30 and 3.30 a.m.

The reporters had many incisive questions about this theory, but the officers were not in the mood to answer any. So, they ignored most of them. Still, some reporters succeeded in asking a few.

The first one asked, "Is this person the only culprit in this heinous crime?"

"Yes," the officer answered.

The second asked, "Did the culprit attack her with any sharp or blunt object, or did he insert the object into the victim's body?"

"According to the postmortem, there was no sign of such activity," the officer replied.

"Then how is it possible? How could such heavy bleeding occur if only one person assaulted her?" the reporter pressed.

The police officers did not answer this question. They collected all the papers, announced the end of the briefing, and moved inside the office. The reporters tried to follow them, some still shouting and asking questions, but the guards did not allow them inside.

Over the next few days, different police officers gave interviews and participated in debates on various news channels. They tried to ignore questions related to the cause of death, and justified the theory of one culprit. They concentrated on the nature of the crime and repeatedly talked about the brutality done to the victim. Their strategy was to avoid unpleasant questions, and they succeeded. It raised the anger of the public against the accused. People organised many marches and protests, demanding capital punishment.

The increasing anger of the public forced the chief minister to form a fast-track court for rapid proceedings. This was declared after meeting the victim's family. He announced a job restoration for the victim's husband, who had been terminated on grounds of corruption, a compensation of Rs 5 lakh to the family, and free education for the victim's children.

Lawyers were unwilling to take the case of the accused, Chatar Singh. At the first hearing, a group of lawyers beat him up. The public wanted a decision without any hearing of the case, which forced the judge to pass an order to provide security to the accused. The judge scolded the police officers for not protecting Singh.

This case headlined for the next two to three weeks. Debates, analyses, reports, stories, and recreations of the incident were prominent in prime-time news. Gradually, other news replaced this incident on news channels, and people forgot about the crime.

The incident resurfaced in the news again after one and a half years when the fast-track court found the accused guilty and sentenced him to capital punishment. Once again, it became a prime-time story for the next few days. This time, it was presented as the victory of truth and justice over crime. The victim's family expressed their gratitude to the respected court, showing their satisfaction with the decision. They hoped the culprit would face his punishment soon.

II

June 1995

It was the monsoon season, and the rain had finally subsided after three consecutive days. Mini's mother sent her to the roof to spread out the clothes to dry. As Mini leaned over the terrace railing, she noticed a family moving into Ramesh Uncle's house across the road. She caught sight of a boy, and he seemed to be one of the new tenants' family members. Ramesh Uncle's house was right across from Mini's, making it easy for her to observe the commotion.

This colony was part of the development association of the city, constructed for low and middle-income groups. Originally, each house had two rooms, one kitchen, and an attached bathroom. Over time, as people's incomes increased, they modified and reconstructed these houses. Some managed to purchase two consecutive houses, converting them into more lavish residences.

Mini's father and Ramesh Uncle were among those who had made such changes. Mini's father had built a big five-room house, while Ramesh Uncle had used the space differently. He had three buffaloes, which he kept in the open area of the second house, while he modified the first one for residential purposes, adding an extra room and kitchen.

For the last several months, Ramesh Uncle had hung a board on the window of this room, advertising "one room set for rent". The day before yesterday, a man and a woman visited Ramesh Uncle's house, perhaps to rent the place, and yesterday they moved in.

It was the first time Mini was seeing someone from this family. Perhaps they were busy adjusting the furniture and luggage. She was surprised at how a family of five could live in such a small room. Her family had a five-room house, yet they felt there was not enough space for everyone.

Mini's father was a government officer, and she was the eldest daughter of the family. They had everything required to be considered a well-to-do family: a colour TV, a refrigerator, a two-wheeler, and fine furniture. At that time, having a colour TV and a refrigerator was a sign of prosperity, and owning a two-wheeler was the icing on the cake. So, this family was one of the prosperous families in the locality.

This boy attracted her attention because of his lean physique. Her brother, four years younger than her, had a more muscular body than this boy. The boy was skinny, but had the right height, almost five feet eleven inches tall. He was standing at the room's exit-cum-entrance door, almost in front of her house's main gate.

Suddenly, a girl of her age appeared at the gate. Perhaps she was his younger sister. Her assumption was correct, because a female voice called them for lunch. Mini smiled at them, and they smiled in reply. It was their first introduction to each other.

***

The boy's name was Shirish. He had a younger sister, a younger brother, and two parents. His father did not have a permanent job. Sometimes he found work, but other times he remained unemployed. Their only furniture was a single bed, which they placed at the room's entrance. During daytime, it served as chairs and a table for guests. A handmade mattress on the floor also served as chairs if there were more guests. They had one aluminium box, which they used as a wardrobe and a study table.

This family was always in an economic crisis. They managed to earn their food and clothes with great difficulty. Very often, they had to skip lunch or dinner, or sometimes go without food for an entire day, making them malnourished and thin.

Despite all odds, Shirish's family was full of life. They enjoyed every possible moment and laughed loudly. They slept late at night because Shirish's father returned home late. If they had something to cook, Shirish's mother would start preparing dinner, and if they had nothing, they skipped it. Soon, their lifestyle became a hot topic of gossip among the ladies of the colony.

Shirish was doing his graduation. He was in his second year of BSc. In the early mornings and evenings, he would be on the roof, studying. He walked from one corner to the other while studying his subject, which left an impression of him as a studious boy.

The image of being a studious boy helped him, as he got some tuitions from the colony's kids. This allowed the family to earn some more money, but they still suffered economically. Mini's brother, Animesh, was one of the kids whom he started teaching. Shirish observed that Animesh was more intelligent compared to the other kids. He was good at maths, which impressed Shirish. This was the reason Shirish spent more time and attention to teach Animesh; he loved teaching him.

Shirish and Animesh had some common points of interest. They were cricket fans. They loved to discuss cricket, cricket players, cricket matches, and play cricket together. Animesh was almost six years younger than Shirish, but both developed a friendly relationship.

As their friendship deepened, they started spending more time together. Animesh knew that Shirish had no television, so he often invited him to his home to watch cricket matches. This way, Shirish met the other family members of Animesh.

Soon, Shirish came to know that Mini was a huge cricket fan. She had excellent knowledge of cricket and cricketers. Sometimes, Shirish could not recognise the players, but Mini talked about everything related to that player. She knew everything about them: their batting style, bowling style, and latest records.

It was unusual for a girl to be a cricket fan, as even the national women's cricket team had no recognition at that time. Girls usually played badminton or skipped rope, and cricket was considered a different world for them. This impressed Shirish.

The age between fifteen and twenty is the age of dreams when emotions run high, and even the smallest things feel larger than life. Mini was the classic girl next door, smart, kind, effortlessly likeable. Her love for cricket had surprised Shirish at first, but it quickly became one of the many things he admired about her.

She had a natural charm that could capture any boy's attention. But in those days, Shirish never thought of her as anything more than a friend. Their families knew each other well, and more importantly, he shared a close bond with her younger brother, something that created an unspoken line he did not consider crossing.

***

One day, Shirish's sister introduced him to one of her friends named Savita. Savita was a tall girl with very sharp features, and one could describe her as beautiful. She offered him a handshake, and it was the first time that Shirish held a girl's hand. His hand shivered when her hand touched his. Savita smiled, and her smile tore his heart.

Savita came to their home very frequently, choosing times when Shirish was at home. Shirish kept an eye on her, and she watched him while talking to the other family members. One day, they caught each other sneaking glances. Shirish's sixth sense told him that it had some meaning, because both experienced the same frequency of emotions.

It was the annual kite-flying day, and Shirish was extremely busy flying a kite. His parents had gone to meet one of their relatives. Suddenly, his sister called him for tea, which irritated him. He scolded his sister, telling her not to disturb him, but she did not listen. He went downstairs to teach her a lesson, but his anger evaporated immediately when he saw Savita waiting for him downstairs, holding two cups of tea. His heart began to beat rapidly.

"She wants to talk to you," his sister said in a low voice.

"Me?"

"Yup!"

He went into the room with Savita. Both sat on the bed, bowing their heads. Both expected the other to start, but nobody did. Time was running out, and Shirish was in a dilemma. He wanted to know what she wanted talk about, and a part of his mind was still on the roof where the kite-flying was at its peak.

"Do you want to say something?" he finally asked, his patience wearing thin.

"Yup! But I don't know where to start," she replied. "Why don't you start?"

"Hmm! Okay. I like you," he said, her last sentence giving him some courage.

"Okay. You like me. Is that enough, or do you want to say something more?"

Shirish wanted to say many things, but his tongue refused to cooperate. He tried to speak but could not utter a single word.

"Do you want to say something?" she asked, enjoying his condition.

"Yes! No!" he stammered, his voice becoming lower with each letter.

"Am I beautiful?" she tried to motivate him.

"Yes, you are magnificent," he said with confidence this time.

She giggled. "Anything else you want to say about me?"

Her giggle gave him more confidence. "You are a good girl."

"How do you know I am a good girl?" She laughed.

"I feel it. Now tell me, what do you think about me?" Shirish asked.

"I think I am in love with you," she confessed, stunning him with this sentence. He did not know how to react. He wanted to sing loudly or dance with her. Sometimes, a person cannot believe in an unexpected gain. *But it was happening to him*. He held her hand to believe what he had heard. She did not resist, so he dared some more and pulled her towards him. She did not resist again. Both felt the heat of each other's bodies. Shirish pulled her again, this time more forcefully, to hug her. Savita was not ready for this, so she resisted. He respected her reticence and let her go. She smiled and thanked him.

The next few days were sunny for him. He built castles in his dreams and broke them when they did not meet his expectations. He waited for her, and when she came, the world became beautiful. He was in another world, forgetting all his problems and deficiencies.

Once, he asked her, "What do you find special in me?"

"Nothing!" she replied with a smile. "You are special because you are ordinary."

It was beyond his imagination, but he was happy. Savita was a girl whom many boys admired. Those boys were rich and had more attractive personalities, but she had chosen him. This gave him a feeling of pride.

***

Savita was a teen and very bubbly by nature. Shirish and she decided to keep their relationship a secret, but as hard as they tried, they failed quickly. Very soon, the aunties of the colony had material for gossip. It started with smiles among the aunties. They passed smiles when they saw them together and soon discussed it in their groups. This whispering proved fatal for their relationship, forcing Savita to stop visiting Shirish's home.

Both Shirish and Savita decided to meet elsewhere. They met twice or thrice in a garden situated at the corner of the city. One day, an incident scared them. It happened when they were sitting in a secluded corner of the park. Suddenly, a few boys appeared from the bushes. They came towards them, and it seemed their intentions were not good. Savita smelled danger, so they stood up and walked away. These boys started chasing them, making cheap and vulgar comments. Savita and Shirish had to run to save themselves from these rowdies.

After this incident, they were scared to meet outside. Savita understood that Shirish did not have a solid physique to fight someone to save her, and it disappointed her. She had seen in movies that even a thin hero could beat ten to twelve goons to protect his love interest. She believed in it blindly, so this incident started to make her doubt Shirish's abilities.

The incident shocked Shirish too. He understood that he had lost his impression on Savita. After that, she never showed willingness to meet him. Shirish realised he was losing her and had to do something if he wanted her in his life. His sister told him that one boy in the colony was chasing Savita frequently. He was trying to attract her attention, and last week, he had bought a stylish and modern motorcycle. It scared Shirish. He knew Savita was a fun-loving girl, and this boy had a bike. This boy definitely had an advantage over him.

One day, they decided to meet outside on Shirish's insistence. In the afternoon, Shirish rode his cycle to a famous temple in the city. This time they were meeting in the temple because of the last scary incident.

It was a hot and humid August day. No rain for five days, and the heat was building up; even though the sun wasn't blazing directly, it was getting troublingly hot. Shirish rode the bicycle for ten kilometres to reach the meeting point, but his tyre flattened midway. He did not find a single repair shop for the next two kilometres and had to drag his cycle along. He arrived late, and his clothes were shabby and untidy.

Savita was furious about the delay. She was not ready to listen to any excuse and continuously shouted at him. Shirish's shabby attire distracted her. She realised she had made a mistake in choosing her love interest.

"Savita!"

Suddenly, a voice attracted her attention. It was the same boy Shirish's sister had told him about. He was on his bike, and invited her for a ride.

Shirish saw a lustre in Savita's eyes. He understood it was the deciding moment, so he held her hand to stop her. The boy came near them and pushed Shirish aside. He held Savita's hand and declared his love for her. Savita didn't react; perhaps she was still in a dilemma. The boy invited her for a bike ride, and this time she couldn't deny him.

Shirish saw Savita going with the boy. This boy had a bike, and Savita was sitting in the back seat. He wanted to stop them, but couldn't, because the boy had a stronger build. He had a faint hope that she would look back, but Savita didn't turn. That was the end of their love story.

It was a shock for Shirish. He believed in love stories in which love won over all obstacles, poverty, and deficiencies. In reality, he had a broken heart, and a feeling that he had lost everything.

III

December 2022

It was one of the foggiest mornings of the season. Mangiram was heading to his field. A disturbed stomach from the previous night had caused him to wake up early. He waited for some time for the visibility to improve, but eventually left home when it didn't seem to happen.

He was passing through an empty field, which was the property of the Forest and Horticulture Department. They had left it unused, and no one took care of it. As a result, many bushes had emerged in this area, some of them taller than a man, almost ten feet tall, making it impossible to see the other side. Suddenly, he noticed that the soil on the side of the road was red—an unusual colour—and it caught his attention. It was not the standard colour of the earth, so it raised suspicion in his mind. He peeped into the bushes but could not see anything, as the visibility was exceptionally low, and the bushes were at least ten feet away from where he stood.

He tried to understand the situation and then decided to investigate further. He tore through the bush with a bamboo stick to reach the area. His front foot slipped when he stepped ahead, and he saw a big pool of blood in front of him. Startled, he had an intuition that something was not right inside the bush. He decided to stop the investigation and stayed there.

After some time, he saw Abdul and Radhe coming towards him. They were also heading to their fields. They stopped and greeted him. Mangiram told them that there was something suspicious in the bushes and showed them the big pool of blood. The sight of the blood scared them all, so they decided to stay and wait for more people to arrive. Soon, more villagers came, and they had enough people to inspect what had happened behind the bushes.

They did not need to do any hard work because they found blood traces just a few steps into the bushes. Initially, it was blood-stained footprints. They walked a few steps more, and these blood-stained footprints changed into thick blood traces and clots. Around 100 metres from the road, they found a dead human body.

***

It was a terrifying scene. Some screamed at the sight, while some vomited. A few ran back to call the police. The police took their time to reach the place of the incident. By then, a mob had gathered there. People clicked photos of the victim, and in the process, they smashed all the bushes and destroyed all pieces of evidence.

The police had to barricade the spot to stop people from reaching the crime scene. Only then, they could start their investigation. The victim was around forty-nine years old. The murderer had cut the victim's significant veins and then forced him to run from the first blood-clot site to inside the bushes. The victim had sat there to rest and could not stand up again due to heavy blood loss. There was whispers in the mob that either this was the work of a witch, or someone had sacrificed the victim for tantric purposes.

Police officers asked the people several times to identify the victim, but no one knew him. Then, the investigating officer noticed that the clothes of the deceased were of a costly brand. He concluded that the victim did not belong to this area, as people here usually did not wear such expensive clothes, deducing that the murderer had brought the victim from somewhere else, possibly kidnapping him.

The investigating officer sent the photos and details of the victim to all the nearby police stations, hoping for a missing person's report filed in any of them. For the next five to six days, the police were clueless and could not find leads from anywhere. As per the rule, they performed the funeral and kept the clothes and belongings found on the victim's body for future identification. Initially, this matter occupied the front pages of almost all newspapers, but slowly it shifted to the second page and finally disappeared from the headlines. The case went into the unsolved list, but one day, a query from a nearby police station forced them to reopen the case again.

The investigating officer asked for information about a missing person, and the in-charge of the police station replied to this query, sending the details of a person named Dr Prakash Kumar who had been missing for more than a month. The investigating officer in Dr Prakash's case sent his photos to this police station.

The investigating officer of the murder case confirmed that the details of both victims had matched. The next day, a woman and a boy came to the police station, and when the clothes and belongings were shown to them, they immediately identified them as the victim's.

The lady started weeping. Officers had some questions, but they had to wait for her to be stable before talking. When she was able to speak, a police officer asked some crucial questions related to the victim's identity, such as name, occupation, and address.

They received some shocking information. The victim was a doctor in a medical college, a professor of anatomy, and his job was performing postmortems. He was a low-profile person and did not engage in private medical practice. He was not very social in behaviour. He was known for his strict routine of home to office and office to family, having no friends and no foes. He had one son, who was nineteen, and his wife was a forty-five-year-old homely lady suffering from gout. She could not stand up immediately if she sat for some time, which was evident from her physique, as she was obese. His son was a brilliant student who had secured the 102nd position in the CPMT exam and was waiting for counselling.

The murderer had killed the victim brutally, but the victim's social and personal life did not indicate any enmity with anyone. The investigating officer was clueless. The police, too, were clueless, and it gave the impression that the officer was doing nothing in this case. The students at the medical college declared a strike until the police found the killer. The strike of medical students disturbed the OPD and regular admissions, with only emergency services being provided. The situation worsened when the Doctor's Association supported the strike and called for agitation against the police's inactivity, threatening to disrupt all medical services.

The police tried their best but didn't find a single clue about the murder. Meanwhile, two patients died in the medical college, and their families blamed the doctors' strike for their untimely deaths. The matter started taking a political angle, and opposition parties joined the strike and agitations. They blamed the state government for the deteriorating condition of law and administration. The matter had started to tarnish the image of the state government, and they were forced to take the agitation and strikes seriously. So, the state government started its effort to control the damage done.

They tightened the screw of the local administration and police; it pressed the panic button of the local authority, and they came in ultra-charged mode. They did their best to find the murderer, or at least to get a lead. They picked everyone whom they supposed to be a suspect. They enquired strictly about each of the suspects and used every possible method. In this exercise, they made a mistake, and an investigating officer beat a suspect badly in police custody. The boy was injured seriously. The doctor saved his life with difficulty.

The next day onwards, it was on the front page of the newspapers. Many organisations started agitating against the police. It resulted in the investigating officer's suspension and transfers of other people associated with the investigation of the murdered doctor's case. The police inquiry stopped with the investigating officer's suspension.

Both matters remained on the newspapers for a few days. Slowly, new news replaced these matters, and people forgot the murder. But someone had decided to shock the city's people and refresh their memories with one more act!

IV

September 1996

Shirish tried to explain his feelings to Savita, but she had already made up her mind to move on. Her rejection hurt him deeply, shaking his belief in emotions and relationships. Wounded, he vowed never to give his heart to anyone again. He became emotionally withdrawn, focusing entirely on his studies and keeping his interactions to a minimum.

Months passed, and gradually, the pain dulled into silence. By the time his second-year annual exams arrived, Shirish had buried his heartbreak beneath routine and restraint. He believed his heart had finally settled: quiet, obedient, and closed to any new stirrings.

But the heart is rarely that simple. Just when he thought he was in control, it betrayed him once more. Quietly and without warning, it began to drift again, reminding him that no oath, however strong, can truly bind what the heart dares to feel.

It was mid-September, and monsoon had almost ended. The earth in the park in front of Shirish's house was still wet from the recent rains, reflected in the irregularly growing grass. The mornings had lost their sweltering heat, and cool breezes made them pleasant.

Every morning, Shirish would study on the roof, walking from one corner to the other during this time. Around 7 a.m., flocks of students would pass in front of his home. They were students from different schools and various classes, usually walking in groups.

She was one of those students, unique because she walked alone even though other students from her school used the same route to catch the bus. Perhaps she was studying in class twelve. He never recognised her among the flock of students until his younger brother drew his attention to her. He had noticed some minute changes in her behaviour whenever she crossed their house. He told Shirish that she seemed uneasy and shy, often bowing her head, with a tiny smile. He was sure that she liked someone in the area, which had forced her to change her behaviour.

At first, Shirish dismissed his brother's observation. He knew very well that around 7 a.m., no one was on the roof or in the streets. It was time to go to school, and all the boys were on the road. There was no one on the roof whom she could like, but he had a thief in his heart who forced him to follow that girl.

Soon, he found that his brother's observation was correct. She did all the activities his brother had described. He tried to trace the man who made her act that way. He tried hard, but it was not easy to trace a girl to find her love interest. Since then, he would go to the roof early in the morning to unveil the mystery. His eyes started tracing her from the street's visible corner and left her at the last point which his eyes could see. He had an exact idea from which house her behaviour changed while crossing. This raised another problem. There was no boy in these four or five houses except him, and this conclusion gave him goosebumps. Was he the object of her interest?

***

The conclusion created unrest in his life. He thought about it all day. Some thoughts increased his heartbeat and assured him that his judgement was correct. In the next instance, his thoughts demoralised him, and he refused his theory. Sometimes he felt positively charged, and sometimes all his energy was drained out.

At night, he decided to test his conclusion, which made him relaxed. He could sleep at night. He had a sound sleep and woke up at around 8 a.m. All the students had gone to their schools. It was not a good morning for him. He was in a bad mood and frustrated about losing the opportunity. Meanwhile, another incident happened that worsened the situation: he fought with his younger sister, and his mother scolded him for his immature behaviour.

He analysed the whole situation again after recovering from his mood. This time, he had more negative thoughts. His belief in his theory was wavering. It became difficult for him to believe that he was the object of her interest. This new conclusion made the day gloomy for him, and a feeling of having lost something started bothering him.

The next day, Shirish woke up early but was reluctant to go to the roof. He brushed his teeth slowly. Suddenly, a voice alerted him, "You are brushing here, and your heroine is passing by."

This made Shirish extra charged. Without thinking, he ran to the roof. She was passing in front of his house. He smiled at her, and she smiled back. This happened unintentionally, but it was one of the happiest moments of his life. He felt like he had won a war or achieved something unique. He walked on the roof for a few more minutes, and when the hangover of his happiness was over, he started thinking about whose voice had alerted him.

It was his father's. He realised he had been caught red-handed. A mixed feeling of shame and guilt troubled him, and he dared not go downstairs. It was June, and the sun was getting hotter. His father understood his feelings and called him downstairs. Shirish entered the room, bowing his head. His father laughed at him, which increased his shame, so he pretended to study.

He felt inexplicable happiness the entire day. By evening, he had no reason to doubt what he had experienced that morning, but as the evening grew darker, uncertainty crept in. He wondered if she had really smiled at him, or if it was his misunderstanding.

He decided to clear up all his doubts the next day. This time, he was confident about executing his plan. The following day, he eagerly waited for her on the roof. Shirish felt that time had stopped for him, and every second felt like a year. Then she appeared from the corner of the street. He smiled at her, but she did not respond.

This was enough to cool down all his excitement. He wanted to do something to draw her attention, but his body refused to obey. He could only wave his hand to say "Hi" with great effort. He was disappointed because she did not show any reaction and walked silently past his house.

Shirish lost all his energy and sat on the boundary wall. Unwillingly, he watched her pass by his house. Suddenly, his heart started beating rapidly. It was hard to believe what he saw. Her hand was behind her, and she was waving in reply. She stopped, placed her foot on the boundary wall of the park, and tied her shoelaces. This time, he saw the smile on her face.

An extreme feeling of happiness washed away his sadness in a moment. He left all his burdens and sorrows behind. He wanted to fly in the sky, feeling lighter than a feather. Once again, the morning became bright for him, and the sunlight felt cooler.

He spent the entire day with this feeling of euphoria. It was the happiest day of his life, but doubt reared its head at night when he was going to sleep. Was she waving her hand to reply to him? Or was there someone else? Or was it just his misunderstanding? He knew there was no one on the roof other than him. His heart knew she was waving at him, but this suspicion created unrest in his life. This unrest did not allow him to sleep. He tried to find a way to confirm.

Finally, he decided to write a letter because, at that time, no one knew about mobile phones. It could be dangerous if this misfired. He knew of many incidents where love letters had been caught, and their writers had faced humiliation. He thought and thought and only wrote a "Hi". He tried hard to write a few more words, but could not dare to execute. Shirish found it safe to write "Hi" because if he had misunderstood her feelings and she took it differently, it could create a mess. He could easily deny that he had written something; and if she agreed to his proposal, this one word would be sufficient.

The next day, he reached the roof early and waited for her. She appeared from the corner of the street. He gathered all his courage, but it became the most challenging task to drop the letter. She was just ten metres away from his house. If he missed, it would be a miss for the day, he thought. Putting all his effort, he dropped the letter from the roof. It waved in the air, and his breath hitched. It seemed like it could go into the neighbour's courtyard. He closed his eyes and prayed to God.

When he opened his eyes, he saw her smiling at his condition. She stopped near the paper, bowed down, pretended to tie her shoelaces, and picked up his one-word love letter. This gave him confidence, and he waved with a smile. Her response was enough to increase his dopamine levels.

It became irrelevant to him what her answer could be. Her smile cleared all his doubts, and he got his answer. It confirmed that she was equally interested in him. The day became longer for him because he didn't go to college and stayed home. He wanted to see her again when she returned from school.

The next day, she dropped a piece of paper a few steps before his house and walked without looking at him. This shocked him, because he had faced failure in his first attempt, and her behaviour scared him. Then he saw a piece of paper on the road. He reached it with a throbbing heart and picked it up. It was a lovely glossy page from a slam book with some questions written on it.

He answered all the questions written on it. He drew small images of hearts and dolls to decorate the page and wrote a note in one corner between these decorations: "Answer all the questions for me too."

The next day, he dropped it in style, and she picked it up. A beautiful and thrilling game had started between them. Each day, one prepared a sheet of questions, talks, and thoughts, which the other replied to the next day. This language of love, though mute, was loud and clear to them, and very cheerful too.

V

November 2019

It was a beautiful day, and Inspector Farrukh Ali was busy with his work. He and his team had caught a gang of thieves, which was a big success for them. This gang was active in many states, and numerous complaints had been registered against them in different police stations across various cities. The police had recovered a pile of stolen items, including TVs, refrigerators, gold and silver jewellery, costly ornaments, and cash. The value of the recovered items was beyond his imagination.

He informed his senior, and was expecting appreciation from them. He received a call from the superintendent and picked it up excitedly. Unfortunately, it was not an appreciation call. The superintendent was in a serious mood and didn't talk about his success; instead, he ordered him to help Ratan Lal as much as possible.

The superintendent's response disappointed him. He swore after putting the receiver on the cradle. This order raised curiosity about Ratan Lal in his mind. He knew the man well; he had a big name in society. He wondered about the nature of the help that had forced him to meet the superintendent.

Ratan Lal was one of the most famous jewellers in the city. He owned the most prominent jewellery store in town and was one of the richest men here, but this was not sufficient to describe his aura. He was also one of the most powerful men in the city. He had many connections with the prominent politicians of the state. These politicians belonged to every political party, ruling and opposition. He was synonymous with power.

Farrukh Ali went to meet Ratan Lal at his home. This was a matter of surprise for those who knew Ratan Lal. He was a man of ethics who had followed a strict routine from the beginning of his career. He reached his office at 11 a.m. sharp and never left before 7 p.m. This suggested that something serious had happened.

The servant took Farrukh Ali to Ratan Lal's room, where he was lying on the bed. A nurse was monitoring his blood pressure. Farrukh Ali felt a mysterious silence in the house; everyone was trying to avoid speaking. Ratan Lal gestured for him to sit on a chair near his bed. Then, he asked the nurse to pause the procedure, held Farrukh Ali's hand, and started weeping.

Farrukh Ali knew well the reality of these so-called big names. They hid many dark stories under their shining names and could go to any extent to keep them hidden. He did not understand how to react to this situation. The atmosphere suggested that something had gone wrong in the family. He patted Ratan Lal's back to console him. Ratan Lal wept for a few minutes, and silence hung heavily in the room.

"May I know what happened, sir, and how I can help you?" Farrukh Ali asked.

"My younger son has been missing for the last ten days, and now his phone is switched off whenever we try to contact him," Ratan Lal replied.

"Sir, your son has been missing for the last ten days, and you did not think it necessary to inform the police?" Farrukh Ali tried to keep his voice from sounding bitter.

But Ratan Lal understood the tone. Nobody dared to talk to him like this in a normal situation, but now he ignored it and clarified why he had not informed the police.

Ratan Lal had two sons and a daughter. Ramesh, his eldest son, was married and had two kids; he helped Ratan Lal in his business. His daughter, Malini, was enrolled in MBBS. He planned to marry her off after she completed her degree, because she had chosen someone as her companion.

Ratan Lal's younger son, Vijay, was pursuing his MBA. He was a loving child of his parents but was not good in studies. Extreme care and pampering had spoilt him, and it showed in his lifestyle. He lived lavishly, wore expensive clothes, and rode a superbike. He also had a personal car which he used to drive to college.

Ratan Lal and his entire family followed the mantra of "simple living, high thinking". He was a strict vegetarian, non-alcoholic, non-smoker, and a God-fearing person. His elder son, Ramesh, had the same habits, though he occasionally consumed alcohol.

His younger son was different. He had all the habits that were against the ethics of his family. He was a party animal and did everything essential for this tag. He was a chain smoker and a perfect example of a drunkard.

Once he started drinking liquor, he drank until the last drop was gone.

Vijay indulged in all types of intoxications. Sometimes he smoked weed or other drugs to get intoxicated. He had a close circle of a few friends who had the same habits. These friends tried to find places where they could spend some days without any restriction. Often this search ended in a farmhouse or an empty bungalow, but sometimes they used vacant buildings for this purpose. Vijay was the leader of this group. He made plans based on the availability of such facilities. This was why he disappeared for some days, but it never exceeded three to four.

The family was accustomed to his habit of disappearing. When they tried to contact him, either the phone rang with no answer, or one of his friends responded that he was sleeping or had gone outside, a perfect reason for not picking up the phone. But they knew he was all right and would return soon.

Apart from this circle of close friends, Vijay knew many people who considered him a friend. Most of them belonged to wealthy families like him, but some were from economically lower classes. They arranged the materials, like weed and other intoxicating drugs, for the group's fun, thinking they were an essential part of the group. But in reality, they were nothing more than flatterers of their wealthier friends.

Vijay had been missing for the last ten days, and the family had no information about him. Initially, they assumed it was his usual disappearing habit, but then there was no word from him for more than seven days. The family tried to contact him but failed, as his number was switched off. This was unusual and raised their concern. They tried to contact all his friends they knew, but no one had any information about him.

The family's worries increased, though they still hoped he would return soon. They enquired about all possible places and called up relatives, but received negative answers. On the ninth day after his disappearance, their hopes began to shatter. Some family members were in favour of seeking police help, but Ratan Lal disagreed. He did not want to involve the law in this matter, as it was a matter of family pride. However, on the tenth day, his patience ran out, and he decided to seek police assistance.

Ratan Lal did not want to make a fuss, so he used his political connections. He called the state's home minister, who then contacted the superintendent of police, who in turn, called Farrukh Ali to handle the matter sensitively and promptly. Farrukh Ali was in charge of the police station in that area, which was why he was at Ratan Lal's home, listening to him.

***

Farrukh Ali noted down every detail about Vijay, including a list of his friends and a photo, and began his investigation with Vijay's close friends. Vijay had a group of four close friends: Ravi, Akbar, Rahul, and Kadir. Vijay, Rahul and Akbar had been classmates since childhood. They had met Ravi and Kadir during their college days. It was an unusual friendship because they did not belong to the same economic class.

After graduation, Vijay, Rahul, and Akbar enrolled in a management course at a high-profile college. Meanwhile, Ravi left his studies to take care of his father's grocery shop, and Kadir continued his post-graduation at the same college. Ravi and Akbar's economic statuses were not equivalent to the other.

While Ravi accepted things as they were, Akbar followed his friends blindly, putting pressure on his family to match the financial status of their friends. Rahul was the son of a businessman dealing in garments, and Kadir's father owned meat factories.

Ravi and Akbar were the odd ones in Vijay's group, making them the natural choice for Farrukh Ali to start the investigation with. Vijay had many friends, but these two were his closest companions. Akbar still studied with him, while Ravi managed his father's grocery shop. According to Farrukh Ali, at least Ravi must not have been in contact with them. He enquired about Vijay's habits and routine from Ravi and Akbar. They answered all the questions confidently but were clueless about his disappearance. They were quite comfortable during the investigation.

Farrukh Ali had a genuine query about why Ravi and Akbar were Vijay's closest friends. He couldn't find an answer to his question about their inclusion in the group. He found no clue but had a strong gut feeling that something was not right. He thought there was something he couldn't put his finger on.

So, he changed his approach. He started asking about their friendship and common interests, which were the reasons for their association. These questions made them uneasy. Sometimes they stammered, and sometimes they tried to avoid answering. It was a clear hint that they were hiding something. He asked the same questions to both, but in different rooms, and found discrepancies in their statements.

These questions made it clear to him that they knew nothing about Vijay's disappearance, but at the same time, he knew that they were not telling the complete truth. His experience told him that these hidden facts had some connection with Vijay's disappearance and that this truth could be helpful in finding Vijay. So, he confiscated their phones, and they revealed some very shocking information.

This information was about Vijay's character. He knew that Vijay indulged in all types of intoxication, including alcohol, drugs, and weed. He knew that spoiled kids usually engaged in such activities. Most of the time, parents know what their kids do, but still try to protect them. However, the videos on the confiscated phones revealed the evil deeds of this specific group of friends.

The phones contained many pornographic videos in which different girls were in objectionable positions with one or more of these five boys. Farrukh Ali understood that they had shot the videos without the girls' consent. Initially, he thought it was a case of pornography, but upon further inquiry, he realised it was a case of breach of trust and blackmail of women.

Farrukh Ali's investigation uncovered the darker side of Vijay's personality. He realised why Ratan Lal was not interested in filing a missing person's report for his beloved son. He was aware of his son's actions and wanted to hide the grim truth about him.

The phones were full of nude photos and videos of different women. Some women were with other men, and Vijay was one of them. Farrukh Ali started asking tough questions, forcing them to reveal the truth. They admitted that they were all involved in this dirty game. Farrukh Ali called Rahul and Kadir to the police station. A single slap was enough to make them confess.

Nothing was common among these five friends except for one shared interest. Vijay, Rahul, and Akbar drew attention from girls and women with their extravagant lifestyle, which was partly fuelled by Vijay's financial support for Akbar.

They trapped them and shot photos and videos when they were in compromising positions. Then, they started blackmailing them. These boys forced the girls to sleep with each member of the group, and it was the beginning of never-ending exploitation.

The list of victims was long. They had already trapped around twenty-five to thirty girls. Further investigation by Farrukh Ali revealed that five girls on the list had died by suicide for fear of social defamation.

It could be a sensitive and high-profile case. Three names in this case belonged to influential families in the state. It could create a quake in state politics. Farrukh Ali discussed the issue with his senior officer. They realised the seriousness of the matter and strictly instructed each member associated with this case not to leak any information to the press or journalists.

An unofficial investigation began to uncover the truth of the case. The loathsome facts were in front of Farrukh Ali, and he didn't want to reveal them, fearing many unpleasant questions. The more he investigated, the more terrifying stories came to light, leading to unrest among the parents of the four culprits.

The parents did everything they could to save their children. They tried to bribe Farrukh Ali to stop the investigation. Although Farrukh Ali was not an honest officer, his conscience did not allow him to take the bribe. He was a God-fearing man and felt that accepting a bribe in this case was against morals and ethics. They gathered at Ratan Lal's home, clamouring for their family's honour and pride. They cried in front of him, begging to be saved from defamation. Ratan Lal was a man of ethics, and doing such things was against his moral values. He took a long time to decide because this was the most challenging choice between ethics and family pride. Finally, the dignity of the family won. He called the state home minister, hesitantly explaining the situation and appealing for help.

The home minister listened patiently and understood the rest. Ratan Lal was the person who had helped him achieve success in politics. Ratan Lal felt low during this conversation. The home minister didn't ask for more details, understanding Ratan Lal's problem, and tried to comfort and assure him of help.

***

Farrukh Ali was in his office when he received a call from the superintendent. He went to the superintendent's office immediately but had to wait for an hour to meet him. The superintendent asked about the progress in Vijay's case. Farrukh Ali tried to explain the new developments without wasting any time, but the officer stopped him. He instructed Farrukh Ali to concentrate on finding Vijay and stop all other time-wasting activities.

Farrukh Ali was surprised. Perhaps the superintendent noticed his expression, for he advised him to conduct a separate investigation in the blackmailing case. The superintendent suggested that he should focus on Ravi and Akbar, who he believed were the masterminds. Farrukh Ali knew it was not a suggestion, but an order disguised as advice to protect the culprits who had influential family members.

Farrukh Ali recognised the political pressure behind the superintendent's words. The superintendent wanted to frame Ravi and Akbar in a blackmailing and assault case while letting Rahul and Kadir go free. This frustrated him. The case had touched his soul, and he wanted to bring all the culprits to justice, but the system prevented him from doing so.

After much thought, Farrukh Ali decided to meet the parents of the girls who had died by suicide. He discussed the situation with them and convinced them to seek justice for their daughters. Two families showed no interest in filing a case against the culprits, as they belonged to powerful families. Two other families did not want to file a complaint due to the fear of social defamation. They said they did not want to disturb the souls of their deceased daughters. Farrukh Ali tried his best to motivate them, but they refused.

This demoralised Farrukh Ali, but he decided to approach the last family. He talked to them and asked them to file a complaint against the culprits. He encouraged them not to let the culprits escape, and it worked. The father of that girl filed an FIR against the five boys. He inspired the other parents to follow his lead. This time, it worked, and the families of the victim girls came together to support the cause. They held a press conference, targeting the influential parents and their undignified sons. They showed the blurred videos in front of the camera, clearly revealing the faces of the culprits instead.

The case immediately attracted media attention. Media vans with reporters gathered in front of the homes of Ratan Lal and the other culprits. Everyone wanted to capture sensational footage. Everything that these families had tried to hide began to be exposed.

Ratan Lal was a close friend of the state's home minister, and the opposition quickly caught on to this fact. They used it to frame the home minister and the chief minister of the state. Images of Ratan Lal and the home minister standing together circulated on social media, showing the close connection between the home minister and Vijay.

The opposition raised the matter loudly in the Legislative Assembly, and the echo of this issue reached the Parliament. It led to loud and noisy debates during Parliamentary sessions, which were put on hold due to this matter. The National Commission for Women took notice and sent a team to investigate. The high court took cognizance of the issue and chided the state government.

There was noise about this case everywhere, but only a few were genuinely interested in fighting for justice. Most people wanted to make louder noise than others. TV channels got material to run 24x7; the opposition used the matter for their political gain; and social media circulated the material for gossip and memes.

The case created uneasiness for the chief minister, and especially the state's home minister. The involvement of the home minister was evident. This matter had ruined the home minister's image in front of the top leadership. However, they did not ask for his resignation because it would send the wrong message about his involvement. So, the party stood by him, but it was clear that his ministerial position was at stake.

To calm the public's anger, the state government referred the case to the CBI. This strategy worked, and the public's anger subsided. Once the public settled down, the matter lost its appeal for news channels, the opposition, and other beneficiaries. Only a few players remained involved: the families of the victims, the police department, some responsible agencies like the National Commission for Women, and the court.

In March 2020, the pandemic sparked global panic, leading to lockdowns worldwide. India was no exception, and on March 22, a nationwide lockdown was declared. Everything came to a standstill, and was delayed or postponed, including the CBI investigation, which was put on hold.

This pause gave the state government an opportunity to reorganise things according to their priorities. The lockdown proved to be a blessing in disguise for the state government, allowing them to reshuffle the administration. As anticipated, Farrukh Ali received his transfer letter, followed by a suspension notice related to an old case. There was also a cabinet reshuffle, and the home minister was reassigned to a less-prominent ministry, effectively becoming the ex-home minister.

The state government did not stop there. Slowly, they changed almost all the administrative staff in the city. The city witnessed the arrival of a young superintendent, a dynamic police officer who was an IPS trainee, bringing with him a lot of public and government expectations.

VI

May 2002

Her father named her Pinki with a lot of love when she was born after her two brothers. Harish, Pinki's father, worked in a private factory where he had to work in shifts. Each shift lasted for a week, alternating between morning and night shifts. He worked in a small-scale pesticide factory, and his duty was to fill bottles with pesticide. Job protocol required him to wear a mask and gloves while on duty. However, Harish found this uncomfortable and inconvenient. He loved the smell of solvents, which was usually kerosene oil, and the coolness of alcoholic solvents. The chemical engineer of the factory, who was also the production in-charge, often scolded him for his life-threatening carelessness.

Harish earned a small salary, and to increase his earnings, he often did overtime. He received a day's salary for working eight hours. This was against the government's wage policy, which stated that eight hours of overtime should equal one and a half days' pay. However, Harish accepted it because it was not easy to find a job in the city where he lived.

Pinki's mother, Rekha, also worked in a small factory near their house. She had to work for nine hours instead of the eight-hour work policy. She accepted this for the same reason as Harish. Despite all odds, both husband and wife made enough to fulfil their needs. They had many dreams for their children. They wanted their elder son to become a police officer, their younger son to become a doctor, and their daughter to become a teacher.

Both husband and wife were not well educated, but they wanted a better future for their children and had their own theories. According to their theory, their elder son was the toughest among their children, making him the best candidate to be a police officer. Their younger son was the most intelligent, and Rekha wanted him to become a doctor who would care for them in their old age. Since their childhood, they had observed that most teachers were women, so they thought teaching was the best job for girls.

Despite all their miseries, they were happy and enjoyed their life, with its ups and downs. They celebrated minor happy moments and bore the saddest moments calmly. However, one day, a steep downturn came in their life, and their wait for the next up became longer and longer.

It was peak time in the factory for pesticide manufacturing. Harish was working for more than twelve hours a day. The supervisor pushed the labourers to maximise production to fulfil orders. Harish was responsible for filling the prepared pesticide into bottles. That day, he noticed that one labourer was feeling unwell, and advised him to go outside for some fresh air to avoid any mishaps.

To maintain the speed of production, Harish took the labourer's seat and started filling the bottles. As usual, he forgot to wear the safety gear, including gloves and a mask, and failed to judge the situation. It was a hot and humid night, and the fumes of the pesticide were stronger than usual. He was sweating profusely, but ignored his body's signals and continued filling. Suddenly, he fell and fainted.

The chemical engineer and production in-charge had already left for home, and there was no decision-maker in the factory at that time. Panic ensued because nobody knew what to do in such a situation. They did what they thought was right: they brought Harish to an open place, and someone splashed water on him to revive him.

Meanwhile, the unit supervisor called the owners and informed them about the situation, but they did not take it seriously. They thought Harish was pretending to take rest. They ordered the supervisor to handle the situation strictly and to resume production, warning him that they would not tolerate reduced output at any cost.

The supervisor followed their instructions. He scolded the labourers gathered around Harish and ordered them to return to work. He then tried to revive Harish but soon realised that he was not pretending. Harish's condition was deteriorating by the minute. The supervisor made another phone call to inform the owners that Harish's condition was severe.

This time, the factory owner realised the situation was not normal. He discussed the matter with the other partners over the phone. They hurriedly reached the factory and instructed the supervisor and manager to take Harish to the nearest hospital. One of them stayed at the factory to manage the work, while the others went to the hospital where Harish was admitted.

Harish was in critical condition and in the ICU. The owners asked the doctor about Harish's health status. The doctor told them they had wasted precious time bringing Harish to the hospital. He scolded them, saying, "We could have definitely saved him if you had brought him here in time."

One of the owners shouted at the manager and the supervisor for their carelessness. This way, he released his guilt, frustration, and feelings of not making the right decision in time. He wanted to show that it was the manager and supervisor who hadn't taken timely action. Both of them accepted the false allegations silently because they had to keep their jobs, as it was difficult for them to find new employment. The owner continued shouting at them, but it didn't leave any impression on the doctor.

It was not the first time that the doctor had encountered such a situation. He was an experienced physician running his nursing home in this industrial area and was aware of the pretentiousness of factory owners. He knew they did it to show their innocence.

After an hour, the doctor called the owners to his chamber and asked, "Have you informed his family about his serious condition?"

"No, we haven't informed his family yet," they replied.

The doctor nodded and then said, "I need to discuss something."

The owners understood the doctor's hint. They instructed the manager and supervisor to wait outside the chamber and told the doctor, "Yes, sir."

The doctor continued, "I know you take all the safety measures on your premises, but these illiterate people do not follow the guidelines properly. This is going to cause problems for you."

"Is everything okay, doctor?" one of them asked worriedly.

"He is not well. I suggest you inform his family. He is on a ventilator, and his recovery is almost impossible. I have to call the police because this is an accidental death," the doctor said, observing the changing expressions on their faces.

"Doctor, please save us. If the police comes, everything will be spoilt. It is peak season, and we must complete the orders. Otherwise, it will be a huge loss for our business," they almost begged.

"Let me see how I can help you. First, inform his family," the doctor said, leaving them in a state of dilemma. They couldn't understand the doctor's intentions, because they had thought he would help them. However, they followed his instructions and told the manager to inform Harish's family about his condition.

The owners discussed the situation and decided to call someone who could persuade the doctor to help them. They contacted a politician they knew well, explained everything, and asked for his assistance. He listened calmly and told them not to worry.

Within fifteen minutes, the politician arrived at the hospital, and in the next five minutes, they were all in the doctor's chamber. This time, the situation was different. The doctor was more friendly and assured them that he would help and rescue them from this predicament. He advised them to manage the police inspector of the industrial area. The politician blinked, indicating he had already handled everything.

Harish's wife and elder son arrived at the hospital, inconsolable, after an hour. They enquired about Harish, but no one answered them. One of the owners intervened and informed Rekha that her husband was seriously ill and the doctor was trying to save his life. He took her to the ICU, to Harish.

Rekha found her husband critically ill and on a ventilator. The doctor told her that Harish had suffered a massive heart attack, leading to cardiac failure. He informed her that there was little hope for recovery. She fell in a state of shock, unable to believe that the man who was fitter than an athlete could have a heart attack.

In the morning, at around 4.15 a.m., Harish took his last breath. Rekha couldn't believe the sudden demise of her husband. Her small world had changed in just a few hours. It took four more hours to get her husband's body. The medical staff didn't allow her to take the body until they had paid the hospital bill and completed the medical and legal formalities.

His son sat helplessly in the hospital corridor. It was a time of grief, but Rekha was busy arranging the money because she didn't have enough money to pay the hospital bill. The factory owner understood her problem and settled the account on her behalf. After the payment, the hospital released the body.

They reached home by 11.30 a.m. and cremated Harish's body by 3 p.m. Their lives had been upended in only twenty-four hours. Rekha and her three children were now left alone to face the challenges of life.

***

Rekha stretched herself to the maximum extent to fulfil her family's needs. Her elder son was sixteen years old, the second son was twelve, and the youngest daughter was only seven. Her elder son left his studies and joined an electrician to learn the trade and support the family. With this, Rekha's dreams began to shatter, but the problems did not end there.

A few friends of Harish started visiting their home very often. Most of the time, these people were drunk. They came to show sympathy to the family, but Rekha could see the lust in their eyes. They boasted about their friendship with Harish and assured Rekha of any help. She had a small house, and these people did not want to leave until late at night. It was difficult to avoid them.

She lived in a colony of semi-literate and illiterate people. Most of the ladies had a great fondness for gossip, and Rekha was the perfect target. Soon, whispers about her character began floating in society. These rumours upset her. She made up her mind to get rid of these people. But one night, she learnt the truth of her husband's death.

Under the influence of alcohol, Naresh, who boasted about being Harish's best friend, made a shocking statement. He told Rekha that her husband had not died of a heart attack. Instead, it was an accident at the factory premises. The next day, Rekha went to the owner's office and started shouting for justice for her dead husband.

The factory owners refused to meet Rekha. They knew she could do nothing except shout. Frustrated, she went to the police station to complain against the factory owner, but the police officer refused to register her complaint. She couldn't understand what she needed to do to get justice for her husband.

One labourer told her about the labour union and advised her to seek their help. Rekha saw a ray of hope and went to the union leader of the industrial estate and told him the entire story. The union leader listened patiently and promised to fight for her. The union leader gathered almost fifty people from the industrial estate and reached the office of the factory owner. This time, they called for a meeting.

In the office, the union leader demanded compensation for Harish's death, a significant amount that could help the family. Rekha wanted the owners to go to jail because her husband's life could have been saved if they had helped him in time. So, she interrupted the union leader and told him her priority. The union leader paused the meeting and came out of the factory owner's office with her. He explained that they had no evidence against the factory owners, and they would easily escape the law. He suggested that if she wanted justice for her husband, she should choose a better option and try to get some money from the owner, which would help her family in the future. Rekha had no choice but to accept this.

The owners called the union leader and discussed the matter in a closed-door meeting. After some time, they called Rekha into the room and asked about the source of her information. She mentioned Naresh's name. They called Naresh into the office and asked about Harish's death. To Rekha's astonishment, Naresh replied that Harish had died due to a heart attack and denied saying anything about Harish's death to Rekha.

Rekha looked at Naresh with wide, horrified eyes. It was hard to believe that he was the same man who had boasted about their friendship the previous night. She tried to remind him again, but Naresh claimed he was under the influence of alcohol. She asked him again, but he did not change his answer. The owner smiled and looked at the union leader, who turned to Rekha for an answer. She was speechless.

"Harish died on your premises. We need compensation," the union leader said firmly.

The owner thought for a moment, then put a bundle of Rs 500 notes on the table and said, "I can only give you this, and I'm giving it because you've come here for compensation, not because we are guilty."

The union leader took the bundle and handed it to Rekha. She had no words to say. She knew the truth, but she could not do anything. She took the bundle and left the matter to divine justice. That night, she was ready with a broom to welcome Harish's so-called friends; the women of the society saw a different side of her. She swept away all the drunkards who claimed to be Harish's friends with the broom.

A few days later, she learned another shocking truth: the deal between the owners and the union leader in the closed chamber. The union leader had settled the matter for Rs 2 lakh and assured the factory owners that Rekha would not come to his office again. She had received only Rs 50,000, and he had kept the remaining money.

***

Eight years passed. Rakesh, Rekha's elder son, started supporting her. He quickly learnt the skills needed and opened a household appliance repair shop. The family became financially stable. Rekha still remembered her husband's dreams. She wanted her second son to become a doctor, but he had already decided on his career. He saw the struggles of his mother and brother and wanted to support them. He had completed class twelve and was in his second year of graduation. He began participating in entrance exams for government services, mainly for clerical-grade and peon positions.

He had a great fascination for government jobs, believing they were the safest option. According to him, no one lost their job, even if they were underperformers. Another benefit was the pension after retirement. This motivated him to apply even more. He did not want to take any risks in his life. He was an intelligent student, and in his second attempt, he cleared an exam for a clerical position. He got his first posting in a different city.

Rekha was satisfied with the justice of life, though her dream remained unfulfilled. She was happy with whatever she got from life and continued working in the factory. She hoped that her daughter would fulfil at least one of her dreams by becoming a teacher. So, she provided all the necessary facilities for her to continue her studies.

Pinki, her daughter, was a good student and secured first division in her high school exams. She was an extroverted girl who loved to live every moment of her life fully, and sometimes she tried to avoid her studies. This puzzled Rekha because she wanted to see her daughter enjoying life like other girls while also concentrating on her studies.

Over the past few days, Rekha had been noticing a change in Pinki's behaviour. She had lost her bubbliness and become abnormally silent. Initially she thought it was a sign of maturity with growing age.

Soon, she noticed that Pinki was scared to go outside. Her maternal instincts alerted her that this was not normal behaviour. She took Pinki into her confidence and asked her what was wrong. Pinki started sobbing. When Rekha asked again, Pinki revealed something that shook her world.

Rajendra, the son of a local leader, had been teasing Pinki for several days. He followed her from home to school and back. He often made cheap comments, gestured lewdly, and sometimes came close to make her uneasy. A few days ago, he stopped her on the way to school and forcefully gave her a letter, demanding an immediate answer and refusing to accept her denial. Rajendra's friends did nothing except laugh at the situation, provoking him not to let her go until he got an answer. Pinki was in the market at the time. It was an odd and unavoidable situation for her. She felt that everyone was laughing at her, and nobody came to help. Rajendra made the world difficult for Pinki.

Rekha was speechless. It was one of the biggest problems she had ever faced. She did not understand how to react or what to do to solve this problem. She wanted to save her daughter but couldn't think of a way. Her family had just overcome the miseries of life. She knew Rakesh would not tolerate this, and it would only escalate the problem.

She consoled Pinki and advised her to take leave for a few days until she found a solution to the problem. This time, life was asking a tough question, and Rekha did not know the answer.

Rekha didn't want Rakesh to know about the matter, so she tried to avoid the problem, but her trick did not work. Rajendra found another way to trouble them. He removed his bike's silencer, making it very noisy, and started roaming in front of their house to attract Pinki's attention. He rode his bike at least three to four times a day through the streets, accelerating to make it noisier whenever he passed their house.

Rumours began to spread among the gossip-loving aunties of the street that Rajendra rode his bike on the road for a girl. This sound was troublesome for the residents of the society, but no one dared to stop him. Everyone in the street feared his father and didn't want to meddle with him, which increased his courage.

One Sunday, Rakesh was at home, and Rajendra crossed the street twice in the morning, irritating him. Rekha understood that if Rakesh stayed home longer, he would get involved in the matter. So, she gave him a list of grocery items and told him to go to the market to purchase them.

Rakesh left the house to go to the market, but unfortunately, Rajendra entered the street at the same time. The sound of the silencer-less bike irritated Rakesh, and he stopped Rajendra when he was passing near him. Rakesh asked him the reason for his frequent visits to the road, and a few people on the street gathered around them.

Rajendra understood the danger. He knew no one dared to attack him individually, but a mob had no face, and they could beat him. Rajendra decided to leave without any resistance. He left the place, but it didn't mean he had left the matter. In the evening, he came with his father, Mahendra Singh.

Mahendra Singh was the local leader of the state's ruling party. He was not in any official position, but he was an important cohort of the MP (Member of Parliament) and MLA (Member of the Legislative

Assembly). He was an influential member of his caste, and could influence their voting patterns.

The members of his caste held the deciding share of voters in this constituency, making him essential for those interested in the city's politics. Both the MP and MLA of the city were overprotective of him, making Mahendra Singh an arrogant person. Coincidentally, the MLA of the constituency was a cabinet minister in the state government.

Mahendra Singh did nothing except politics, which for him meant brokering for his leader. He arranged "settings" between the client and his leader, which involved commissions in tenders, administrative work, and all government examination results where the leader had direct involvement. The client was a contractor or person needing the political leader's interference. As a professional, he declared himself a leader-cum-property dealer.

This was why he had good relationships with people in the city's administration and police department. Many influential people liked to keep him in their contacts. He could gather prominent community members with a single call, and he loved to keep people around him to show his power, which scared the commoners.

Mahendra Singh was in the street, challenging the people who had dared to stop his son in the morning. Those who had shown their courage that morning did not come out when Mahendra Singh reached the street and started shouting. He decided to leave when he thought he had sufficiently threatened the residents.

Rajendra Singh was not satisfied with this. He was annoyed with Rakesh because he felt insulted. He wanted to teach that insolent Rakesh a lesson for daring to stop him. He started hurling abuses in front of Rakesh's house, scaring the family, who did not open the door. This enraged him, and he kicked the door and threw stones.

Rajendra's madness scared Mahendra Singh too. He had not expected such a reaction from his son. He instructed his men to control Rajendra and take him home. They managed him with difficulty, as he became vigorous when he saw them. He wanted to take revenge for his insult.

The next day, Rajendra stopped Rakesh on the way to his shop. He was not alone, and had ten to twenty friends with him. He threatened Rakesh for his actions the previous day. Rakesh knew he couldn't fight these goons, so he apologised and tried to leave. But Rajendra didn't want to let him go easily and provoked him further by saying filthy words about his sister.

This provoked Rakesh, but he managed to keep himself calm. He asked Rajendra the reason for his anger and tried to stop him from speaking so lewdly about Pinki. But Rajendra had no intention to listen, and used Rakesh's objection as a reason to start lynching him. They beat Rakesh badly and left him seriously injured. Rajendra Singh did not stop there. He knew his father's reach in political circles, which made him overconfident. He returned to the street, challenged the residents, but nobody came out. This time, it quenched his thirst for revenge. He then kicked Rekha's door and informed her in a warning tone to see her son, who was lying injured on the road.

This information scared Rekha. She hurriedly reached the place where Rakesh was lying injured. No one came to help him, although some shopkeepers gave him water to drink. She asked for help from the people present in the market, but no one heard her appeal. They didn't want to challenge Rajendra Singh or get involved in the problems created by the police.

Rekha's patience was exhausted. She started cursing the shopkeepers, but it didn't leave any impression on them. Someone suggested that she should take Rakesh to the hospital, but she didn't listen to them. She went to the police station to lodge an FIR against Rajendra Singh. Some people accompanied her: some to support her and some to see the drama.

The police inspector refused to file the FIR, saying that she was trying to trap an innocent boy to extort money. He shouted at her when she persisted in her demand. The people who had come with her started leaving when they saw the inspector's behaviour, and the inspector dispelled the rest soon after.

Rekha did not understand what to do in this situation. Almost all the people who had come with her left, and the one or two who were still there remained silent. She came out of the police station, and one of them suggested she go to the superintendent's office.

Rekha had no other option, so she went to the superintendent with her severely injured son. Fortunately, the superintendent was in the office. He listened to her problem, understood the matter, arranged medical help for Rakesh, and reprimanded the inspector for his misbehaviour. He instructed the inspector to lodge an FIR immediately and take action against the culprit.

Only then did the inspector file her FIR and arrest Rajendra Singh. But this did not comfort Rekha, and she was highly disappointed to see how the police treated Rajendra. They provided him with everything on demand. The police officer edited her FIR and filed it under lighter sections of the law. She understood she could not get justice from this biased officer.

In the evening, Mahendra Singh came to her house with some influential people from society. His behaviour was completely different from the previous night. He apologised for his misbehaviour and requested her to withdraw her complaint, pleading that it would ruin his son's future. They people pressured her to compromise and withdraw her report. She had seen the police's behaviour that afternoon and had no hope from the law, but her family would be in danger if she withdrew her complaint. She expressed her fear to these so-called elderly and influential persons.

Mahendra Singh promised to bear all the medical expenses for her son and guaranteed his son's future behaviour. Rekha showed the letter Rajendra Singh had given to Pinki. Mahendra Singh promised in front of everyone that his son would never come near her daughter and would maintain a distance of 100 metres in the future. Only then did Rekha agree to compromise with him.

The next day, Mahendra Singh gave Rekha Rs 75,000 at the police station to treat her son. Rekha agreed to compromise when Mahendra Singh wrote everything on paper. One copy of the agreement was submitted to the police station, and one copy each was given to both parties.

***

Once again, life slowly returned to normal for Rekha's family. Pinki started going back to school. Rakesh's wounds and fractures took time to heal. Over the past few years, he had become the main earner for the family, so his injuries created a financial crisis. Rajesh, Rekha's second son, did his best to support the family, but his salary was not enough to cover all their expenses.

Six months passed, and during this time, Rajendra Singh did not cause any trouble. Rekha's family began to forget the painful past. They started believing that Mahendra Singh was keeping his word and had controlled his son. Rakesh was recovering well and had returned to work.

But one day, an incident shattered all their hopes. Rekha was returning home after buying groceries when she saw Rajendra Singh coming out of her house. She felt a wave of fear and sensed something wrong. She hurried inside and found Pinki standing still, shocked. Pinki's clothes were not properly worn, and she tried to fix her dress when she saw Rekha. Tears started rolling down her face.

Rekha immediately understood what had happened. Pinki's condition said it all. Rekha stood speechless, not knowing how to react. Fear and helplessness filled her heart. One of her sons had just recovered from injuries, and she had seen before that no one came forward to help her family, not even the police, who always favoured Mahendra Singh.

Thinking for a moment, she asked Pinki to fix her clothes and told her not to mention anything to Rakesh. Then, Rekha decided to meet Mahendra Singh and complain about his son's actions. But when she reached his house, Mahendra's wife started shouting at her, calling Pinki characterless and blaming her for trapping Rajendra. She told her husband not to listen to Rekha. Mahendra Singh threw a bundle of money at Rekha and asked her to leave.

It was a deep insult. Mahendra Singh was trying to put a price on their dignity. He threatened Rekha not to go to the police and forced the money into her hands, warning her about the shame it would bring to her daughter's name. Rekha, feeling helpless but firm, refused the money and requested him to control his son. Mahendra Singh gave her false assurances that he would handle it.

Rekha tried to convince Pinki to forget the incident like a bad dream. But some nightmares do not end so easily. Rajendra Singh had now realised the helplessness of Rekha's family, and it made him even bolder.

One evening, he again forced his way into Rekha's house. Luckily, Rekha was home. When he tried to molest Pinki, both mother and daughter fought back bravely and did not let him succeed. His failure made him furious. He attacked Rekha with a knife and injured her badly.

This time, Rekha went straight to the police station. However, the same officer on duty refused to register her complaint again. He advised her to settle the matter quietly, warning her about Mahendra Singh's political power and the troubles of a long legal fight. But Rekha was determined not to compromise this time. She warned the officer that if he did not accept her complaint, she would approach his senior officers. The officer, knowing she was capable of doing it, finally handed her a paper and a pen to write the complaint.

Rekha wrote down the entire incident in detail. After reading it, the officer refused to accept her version and tried to force her to change it. When she refused, he shouted at her and tried to scare her, but Rekha stood firm and did not change a single word. Frustrated, he threw the paper on the desk of the station clerk and instructed him to file it. He warned Rekha not to come back to the police station again.

The next day, Mahendra Singh came to Rekha's house with some influential elders from the community to pressure her into withdrawing the complaint. They pleaded, threatened, cursed, and even offered money, but Rekha did not give in. She refused to take back her complaint.

Finally, the police arrested Rajendra Singh. The inspector warned Rekha after the arrest, making it clear that he would not have arrested Rajendra had the superintendent not forced him to do so.

Rajendra Singh was presented in court the next day. His lawyer pleaded for bail, claiming that Rajendra was a minor. They showed the court a horoscope as a proof of his age, but the magistrate refused to accept it and asked for a birth certificate or any other official document. The lawyer then argued that the birth certificate had a clerical mistake. The magistrate laughed at the weak excuse and ordered them to bring proper proof. When the lawyer requested medical testing to prove Rajendra's age, the judge rejected the request. He ruled that Rajendra Singh was not a minor, denied his bail, and sent him to jail.

The next hearing was set for three months later, which meant Rajendra would stay in jail for at least that long. Rekha finally felt a little relief and believed that this time, she might get justice.

But trouble was not over yet.

One day, Pinki did not return home at her usual time. Rekha waited the whole afternoon, growing more anxious by the minute. She feared Mahendra Singh might have done something. Around 6 p.m., when

Pinki still hadn't come back, she informed Rakesh. Rakesh also became worried. Together, they searched for Pinki, asking her friends and relatives if anyone had seen her.

As night fell, their fear deepened. They finally decided to seek police help and went to the police station to report that Pinki was missing. But again, they faced the same rude officer, who this time flatly refused to register the report.

"You have no other work! You come here every other day to make false complaints!" the inspector shouted at them.

"Sir, my daughter hasn't come home yet! Please help us find her," Rekha pleaded.

"What can I do? She must have run away with someone. Don't create a scene, she will return in a few days," the inspector scolded them.

"Sir, she is not that kind of a girl. Please file our report," Rekha requested again.

"Get out of here, or I will beat you if you come back!" the inspector shouted.

Despite their repeated requests, the inspector ignored them. Realising that he would not help, Rekha and Rakesh left the police station in disappointment and continued their search for Pinki on their own.

The family spent a sleepless night, trying to find any information about Pinki, but got no positive news. Deep fear settled in their hearts. The next morning, they went back to the police station. Luckily, the station in-charge was not there. They sighed in relief and begged a sub-inspector to file their report. The sub-inspector, feeling pity for them, agreed to help.

Suddenly, the station in-charge returned. Seeing Rekha and Rakesh there, he became furious and started abusing them. Rekha firmly told him that she would not leave the station until the report was filed. This angered him even more, and he raised his lathi to beat them. The constable and sub-inspector quickly intervened and stopped him.

At that moment, a journalist, who had come to gather routine news, witnessed the scene. Curious, he asked a constable about the matter and realised it could be a big story. He approached Rekha and Rakesh for details. Rekha, crying, explained everything: from the misbehaviour of the station in-charge to Pinki's disappearance.

The next day, the news was on the front page of the city section. The journalist had written a detailed story, mentioning the names of Pinki and Rekha, which suddenly made their family the centre of attention. People who already knew the family started asking questions again and again. It was humiliating and painful for them. They had no way to escape this unwanted attention, and Pinki was still missing.

However, the news helped them too. The police superintendent took notice and asked the station in-charge about the case. The inspector tried to mislead him, even mentioning the previous incident by mistake. The superintendent called Rekha to his office for clarification. She told him everything, including the non-cooperation of the inspector.

The superintendent was furious. He scolded the inspector for his behaviour and ordered him to immediately file the missing person's report and start searching for Pinki.

Another day passed. With every passing hour, hope for Pinki's return faded. That night, a constable arrived at Rekha's house with some news. A seriously injured, unconscious girl had been found near the bushes by the railway track. The description matched Pinki's.

They rushed to the hospital with the constable. The girl was in the ICU, unconscious and in a very critical condition. Doctors allowed Rekha to see her for identification. One look was enough: it was Pinki.

Scars all over her body told the story of the brutal torture she had suffered. The medical report confirmed that she had been gang-raped multiple times. She also had a fractured rib and a broken bone in her hand. The doctors were fighting to save her, and the next forty-eight hours were critical.

The same journalist who had first reported the case now had fresh news for the next few days. The incident attracted huge public attention. The police department was under heavy pressure. The superintendent, already unhappy with the station in-charge, recommended his suspension. It was approved immediately.

Meanwhile, Pinki fought bravely for her life and defeated death on the third day. Once she regained consciousness, her recovery was quick. But the family, though relieved, had lost their faith in the system.

The superintendent personally visited them, consoled them, and assured them of full justice. He promised to personally monitor the investigation and not let any culprit escape.

Once Pinki was declared stable, she gave her statement to the police. She revealed the whole truth. Mahendra Singh had kidnapped her to avenge his son's arrest. With the help of two friends, he abducted her while she was returning from school. They kept her locked in an abandoned house near the railway tracks.

There, the three men raped her repeatedly. They tortured her to "teach her a lesson". Their original plan was to keep her captive for a few more days, but after the missing person's report was filed and the news spread, they panicked. They decided to throw her near the railway tracks and stage her death as a suicide. Pinki didn't know how she survived, but somehow their plan failed.

News of Pinki's suffering spread across the city, sparking public anger. The police's earlier negligence added fuel to the fire. Many student groups, organisations, and business communities demanded action and justice.

With the investigating staff replaced, results started coming quickly. Based on Pinki's statement, the police arrested Mahendra Singh. He was presented before the court. His lawyer tried to get bail, but the court rejected the plea and sent Mahendra Singh to police remand for fifteen days for further investigation.

Mahendra Singh couldn't withstand the pressure of police interrogation for more than two hours. He broke down and confessed everything, confirming Pinki's statement. In his confession, he admitted to committing the crime with his friends, driven by a burning desire for revenge against Rekha's family.

He told the police that he was enraged when they filed an FIR against his son. "I was ready to pay any amount for his release," he said, "but they still went ahead and got him arrested." His voice dripped with resentment. In his eyes, it wasn't his son who had done wrong, it was Rekha's family who had dared to demand justice. He arrogantly admitted that he had counted on manipulating the police like he always had. But the superintendent's unexpected involvement had destroyed all his plans. The most chilling part of his confession was this:

Mahendra Singh still believed his son had done nothing wrong.

This time, however, the police didn't repeat their earlier mistakes. The case was airtight. Mahendra Singh was charged with heinous crimes, and the law showed no mercy. Both father and son ended up behind bars; a corrupt inspector, a spoilt son, and a vengeful father had nearly destroyed not just one, but two families.

But for Rekha's family, the suffering didn't end there.

Those who had once sided with Mahendra Singh now turned hostile towards Rekha and her children. Whispers followed them everywhere. Even people who had nothing to do with either family began questioning them, not out of curiosity, but with the intention to shame. They already knew the truth but still asked the same painful questions over and over. Faced with constant humiliation and a community that had turned cruel, Rekha made a decision. She sold their house and moved to the city where her younger son, Rajesh, lived.

In the new city, Rekha bought a small house. It wasn't much, but it gave them a fresh start, a chance to heal. Still, the memories clung like shadows. The past had left scars that didn't fade easily. Life ahead was uncertain. Rekha and her sons needed time to recover. But Pinki? Pinki might need a lifetime to forget what she had endured.

One evening, Rakesh and Rajesh sat beside her in the quietude of their new home. Rajesh gently said,

"Sister, I cannot change your past. But I'll do everything I can to shape your future. Start studying again. Do what you love. Dream again." Then he turned to Rakesh and added, "Brother, I chose a safe job because I was afraid of taking risks. But now I realise, you're always at risk if you're weak. I want to become a police officer. I'll try my best."

VII

August 2020

The Central Bureau of Investigation (CBI) started digging into all the graves and every secret buried within them. The four boys were now in CBI custody. Their families, who once attempted to suppress the case, were now desperately trying to save their sons from severe charges. It was ironic; they still fought not for justice, but to protect the so-called honour of their families. They even tried to influence the direction of the investigation.

As the CBI deepened its probe, other agencies joined. Since the case involved the misuse of drugs, the Narcotics Bureau also stepped in. Although these boys were not part of any organised drug racket, the presence of drugs made them easy targets; and the agencies had no intention of letting them off lightly. They tightened their grip around them.

Meanwhile, Ratan Lal found himself in double trouble. While the CBI treated his son, Vijay, as an absconder, Ratan Lal knew the bitter truth: his son was genuinely missing. He approached the local police for help, but they were reluctant to interfere in a CBI investigation. At the same time, the CBI kept pressuring the family to produce Vijay.

The CBI officers left no stone unturned. Almost every alternate day, someone from the agency would turn up either at Ratan Lal's residence or his business premises. It was relentless harassment. A man who had spent his entire life with dignity was now facing daily humiliation, before his own family, his neighbours, and his customers. For the first time in his life, he felt truly helpless. He had always ensured that neither he nor his family would have to step inside a police station or courtroom. Now, CBI raids had become an everyday affair at his home and office.

The case not only shattered his personal reputation, but also destroyed his political influence. The politicians he had once supported turned their backs on him. Even his closest friend, who once held the powerful home ministry portfolio, lost his position while trying to help him. Business took a nosedive as well; people in the city started avoiding his establishments.

But Ratan Lal's misfortune didn't end there. Vijay was the pampered child of both parents. His mother, unable to bear the agony of his disappearance, gradually lost her health and, one night, silently passed away. After her funeral, a grief-stricken Ratan Lal handed over the business to his elder son and decided to fight: for his rights, and for the truth.

He went to Delhi and met the secretary of the home minister. Despite his troubles, Ratan Lal still had some political connections; he knew that in politics, there were no permanent friends or enemies. He pleaded with the secretary to arrange a meeting with the home minister. The secretary smiled and said, "It's not possible right now, but I'll try to help you in another way."

The secretary made a call and then assured him, "From today, no officer will come to your house or office."

"Thank you, Shukla ji," Ratan Lal expressed gratefully. "But my real request is that the CBI must acknowledge my son as missing, not absconding."

Shukla replied, "Let the officers complete their work. Right now, the tide is against you. Let the emotions settle, then I'll speak to them."

True to his word, the harassment raids stopped. However, the CBI continued summoning Ratan Lal and his elder son regularly. The agency still firmly believed that Vijay was absconding, and that the family was hiding him. Ironically, Ratan Lal's political attempts to seek help only deepened the CBI's suspicion. The officers no longer used physical pressure, but they had their own methods of harassment, and they used them expertly.

Still, Ratan Lal stayed strong. He was ready to face any consequence, still holding on to the hope that if the police treated Vijay as missing rather than absconding, they might genuinely try to find him.

The investigation dragged on for nearly eighteen months. Finally, the CBI filed a charge sheet against the four boys they had in custody, and against Vijay, who was listed as absconding.

Determined, Ratan Lal hired a team of lawyers. They fought in court to have Vijay officially recognised as missing. His lawyer filed an appeal requesting the court to instruct the local police to register a missing person's report.

The court found his request genuine and ordered the local police to submit the status of Vijay's missing person's report by the next hearing. For the first time in months, Ratan Lal had heard good news.

The police resumed their investigation from where they had left off. However, a lot of precious time had been lost, and with it, critical evidence and leads.

Meanwhile, the CBI's court proceedings continued. The agency presented solid evidence and a detailed sequence of events. They successfully conveyed the seriousness of the crimes to the court. In the end, the court found all four boys guilty and sentenced them to seven years in prison. The court also instructed the local police to continue searching for Vijay and produce him in court.

Thus, the case reached its conclusion, but the truth remained bitter.

In reality, this case never needed CBI intervention. It was handed over to the agency purely for political damage control. And in that, the political leadership succeeded.

***

The court had instructed the police to find Ratan Lal's son, but it proved to be only a temporary relief. The police failed to trace his whereabouts. Six more months passed, and still, neither the police nor anyone else had any clue about Vijay. Even Ratan Lal, who had been tirelessly running from one police officer to another, began to lose hope.

Yet, the father in him refused to believe that his son would never return. The police, however, had started treating the case as dead. They avoided answering Ratan Lal's questions, giving him only vague assurances. Their apathy and carelessness hurt him more than their failure.

One day, Ratan Lal heard about a major change in the city's police department. Several officers had been transferred, and new ones had joined. He heard promising things about the new superintendent of police. Gathering the last bits of his courage, he went to meet the new SP and narrated his story.

The very next day, a new investigating officer visited Ratan Lal's home. He informed him that the superintendent had taken a personal interest in the case. The officer collected as much information as possible and decided to start the investigation afresh. He circulated Vijay's photo in nearby police stations and also requested information about any unidentified bodies recovered in the last two years.

This fresh start soon bore fruit, but the answer it brought was heartbreaking.

The officer found information about three unidentified bodies matching Vijay's description. He called Ratan Lal to the police station and informed him of the findings. He suggested that Ratan Lal visit the concerned police stations for identification.

Finally, the moment arrived. At the second police station, Ratan Lal identified a T-shirt and a wristwatch that belonged to Vijay. The search he had carried on for so many painful months ended there. The patience he had shown for nearly three years broke. His emotions poured out in tears: he sobbed quietly, then wept aloud, and finally cried uncontrollably.

The investigator gathered the case details from the police station in-charge. Vijay had been brutally murdered. His body was recovered from a dense forest ridge on the outskirts of the city three years earlier, just a few days after he went missing. The police suspected that he was kidnapped and taken to the crime scene. The killer had severed major veins in his thighs and arms, leaving him to die from massive blood loss. When the police found his body, it was soaked in blood, and the crime scene bore marks of a desperate struggle before death.

The police had tried their best to identify the body at the time, but had failed due to lockdowns during COVID-19's first and second waves. With no other option, they conducted a funeral for the unclaimed body. An NGO, which handled such cases, later immersed the ashes in the river as part of their regular procedure for abandoned funerals.

Ratan Lal's relentless search had ended, but all that remained in his hands was emptiness.

He couldn't perform Vijay's last rites. He didn't even have his ashes to mourn.

Grieving, Ratan Lal travelled to Haridwar, the sacred city on the banks of the Ganga.

He carried with him the T-shirt and watch—Vijay's last belongings that he possessed—to feel his son one last time. Sitting by the river, with trembling hands, he held the items close to his heart. Then, slowly, he let them drift into the holy waters.

As the river carried them away, Ratan Lal whispered a final goodbye to his beloved son.

VIII

February 1997

The language of love is boisterous. Whether someone speaks a word or remains silent, it loudly reveals those who are in love. Shirish continued his strict daily routine of going upstairs and waiting for her. They were extremely cautious in expressing their feelings. Communicating only through sign language from opposite corners of the street, their silent conversation ended at the second corner where she disappeared from his sight.

Shirish never dared to meet her outside because he carried the bitter memory of a past affair.

This ten-minute love story continued for more than two months, and both firmly believed that no one had any idea about their relationship.

Gautam and Tinku lived in the houses at the corner of the street. They were neighbours who rarely went to school. One day, as Shirish was returning home from college, they stopped him, inviting him to play badminton with them. Initially, he refused, but after some insistence, he agreed to join them in the evening.

That evening, he reached the agreed place, a square plot fenced all around where they had prepared a badminton court. There he found four more boys. They divided themselves into pairs, forming three teams. Their gameplay amazed Shirish. He had never seen anyone play badminton like them, smashing the shuttlecock with full power and picking delicate drop shots with lightning speed. Until that moment, he had always considered badminton a child's game. But these boys changed his perception.

Suddenly, Tinku offered Shirish his racquet, urging him to join. Though Shirish believed he was a decent player, seeing their skill made him hesitate. To avoid humiliation, he declared himself a beginner. Tinku smiled and handed him the racquet.

Reluctantly, Shirish started playing, soon realising he was a complete novice around them.

Surprisingly, every time he hit a shot, no matter how poor, they clapped enthusiastically, as if he had played brilliantly. He understood the reason behind their exaggerated encouragement later.

He began playing badminton with them regularly. Their applause made him believe he was improving rapidly. Another reason he kept coming back was that, while everyone contributed money to buy shuttlecocks and new racquets, no one ever asked him for any money, a relief for Shirish, who hardly had enough to spare.

One day, as he was about to leave for the game, his sister stopped him. Her unusual behaviour puzzled him. He asked why, but she remained silent and instead handed him a letter.

It was a love letter written by Pankaj, the leader of the group, and addressed to his sister.

Now Shirish understood the real reason behind the boys' generosity. Anger surged inside him.

He wanted to confront them immediately, but his sister stopped him, urging him to calm down, but he wasn't ready to listen.

"How dare he write a letter to you!" he shouted.

"Brother, just ignore him," she tried to soothe him.

"He should not have done that! I'll teach him a lesson!" he fumed.

"Why are you so angry?" she asked, irritation creeping into her voice. "Just because someone wrote a letter to your sister? You can write letters to someone, and that's okay, but when others do the same, you want to fight them?"

Her words hit him hard. He realised there was no real difference between himself and those boys. Guilt troubled him. For the next two days, Shirish didn't go up to the roof. Once again, it was his sister who opened his eyes with her wisdom.

When she enquired about his sudden disappearance from the roof, he confessed his dilemma and guilt. Laughing, she said, "Has she ever given your letter to her parents or complained about your misbehaviour?"

"No," he admitted.

"That's the difference between her and me," she explained. "She likes you. These boys only irritate me."

Her words cleared his confusion. The next day, Shirish couldn't wait to see her. For the first time in three months, he waited for her not on the roof but at the gate, with a letter in his hand. As she passed, he dropped the letter near her. She bent down, pretending to tie her laces, and picked up the note.

Shirish smiled at her; she returned the smile. They forgot that it wasn't morning, but noon. They didn't realise their mistake at that moment.

The next morning, when Shirish went up to the roof, he wasn't alone. His neighbours, Arun, Sanjay, and Umesh, were also on their roofs. Vimal and Dheeraj roamed the street below. He immediately understood: this was the side-effect of yesterday's mistake.

At the same time, she appeared at the street corner. Noticing the boys around, she became cautious. Shirish, too, changed his body language, pretending to be busy studying on the roof, as if he hadn't even seen her. She walked past, without dropping the letter this time.

They repeated the same routine for the next few days, carefully hiding their affection, until finally, the boys who had been spying on them lost interest and stopped watching. In her next letter, she wrote that she wanted to meet him somewhere else. She explained that it was too risky to continue like this. She shared the address of her school and suggested meeting near it, mentioning that since she was the only girl from their locality attending that school, the chances of being seen were very slim. She had a fifteen-minute window before her school started and wanted to use that time to meet him.

Her school was about four kilometres from Shirish's college. Still, without hesitation, he began cycling an extra eight kilometres every day just to see her. But to do so, he had to miss his chemistry class. He went there twice or thrice and soon realised that this arrangement wasn't practical. Not only was he exhausted by the time he got there, but his clothes were also shabby and soaked in sweat—the very reasons he had lost his first girlfriend. He didn't want to repeat the same mistake.

One day, when they sat together, he softly told her his problem. He explained that he couldn't afford to miss his chemistry classes any more. She listened quietly and, with a gentle smile, told him to prioritise his studies and attend his class.

Once again, the game of hide-and-seek resumed between them. But this time, a few more players had joined the game. Some neighbours noticed the silent exchange of letters between Shirish and the girl. One evening, Sanjay, Umesh, and Arun called Shirish for a walk. On the way, they began casually discussing girlfriends and relationships, and then, slowly, came to the real reason for inviting him.

They wanted to know about his relationship with the girl. Shirish, sensing their intention, feigned ignorance. They told him that Sanjay was interested in her. If Shirish was already in a relationship with her, Sanjay would not interfere, but they needed to know the truth.

Shirish understood the trap they were trying to set. He remained firm, denying any involvement. When they failed to get a straight answer, they switched tactics. They pressured him to accept the girl as his sister, thinking this would clear Sanjay's path. Shirish hesitated. But realising they would keep creating problems, he finally gave in and agreed, just to be left alone.

He thought the matter was settled. But he had no idea that bigger troubles were about to begin. Two days later, the landlord, furious, called Shirish's father for a serious talk. He angrily accused Shirish of spoiling the decorum of the neighbourhood, warning that his behaviour could mislead the other children. Shirish's father tried to reason with him, saying that this kind of behaviour was natural at that age, but the landlord was in no mood to listen.

***

It was the fifth day she hadn't appeared on the street to go to school. A growing uneasiness gnawed at Shirish. His intuition whispered that something was wrong, and he refused to dismiss it as a usual absence.

Unable to sit with the discomfort, he decided to go to her school. One afternoon, he cycled to her school, scanning the faces anxiously. He didn't find her. However, he recognised some of her friends from the times he had seen them together. Summoning all his courage, he approached one of them and asked about her. The girl gave him an irritated look at first, but then, recognising him faintly, she replied, "She hasn't been coming to school for the past five or six days."

He consoled himself with the thought that she might be ill, but no reassurance could ease the heaviness in his heart. That night, another painful realisation struck him: he knew so much about her, her name, her hobbies, her favourite books, yet none of it could help him find her now.

He didn't even know where she lived. In a town so vast, finding her would be like searching for a needle in a haystack. Days turned into weeks. Almost a month passed. She didn't return to the street. Shirish's hope thinned, and he began to believe she never would.

One day, as he was returning from college, destiny played a cruel trick. He saw her. She was getting down from a school bus. His heart pounded. Without thinking, he ran home, tossed his bag on to the bed, and sprinted to the rooftop. Frantically, he scribbled a letter, pouring out his anguish, asking why she had disappeared. He waited on the roof for over an hour, hoping, praying. He knew it didn't take that long to reach home from the bus stop. But still, he waited.

She never came. Crushed, he realised she must have changed her route home. Maybe their relationship was over. The thought pierced deep into his soul. But he couldn't accept it without knowing the reason. He couldn't stop her at the bus stop, because that would humiliate her—something his upbringing would never allow.

So, he went back to her school. She was standing with her friends, waiting for the bus. He wanted to approach her, but his feet froze. One of her friends pointed to him. She noticed him, hesitated, then, gathering courage, walked towards him. Silently, she led him to an empty playground at a little distance from the others.

Facing him, she smiled faintly and took his hand. Her fingers trembled. Her eyes glistened with unshed tears.

"Please forget me," she whispered.

"Why?" was all that Shirish could manage.

"Because I can't fight my family," she said, her voice trembling. "They will never allow me to have a relationship with you."

"But... how do they even know about us? Once I get a job, I'll convince them, I promise," he pleaded.

"They know everything," she said. "Someone sent them a letter... revealing everything."

"Who could do that?" he muttered in disbelief.

"I don't know," she said, brushing a tear away. "But now I have two choices: marry someone they choose for me, or continue with my studies... alone. I choose to study. I have no other option."

"We can manage somehow!" he said desperately. "Please... don't leave me."

She looked at him with infinite sadness and said, "Then take me away. Far from here. From them."

A heavy silence hung between them.

"Where would we go?" he said after a while. "My family has placed all their hopes in me. How can I abandon them?"

She smiled through her tears.

"Then leave me," she said softly. "Stay with your family. And I'll try to find happiness with mine."

Her bus arrived in the distance. Before she left, she stood on her toes, kissed him lightly on the cheek, and said, "I know you're a good man. I trust you'll understand."

Shirish stood frozen, watching her walk away. He waited, aching, hoping she would turn back. If she turned back even once, he believed, it would mean she still belonged to him. But she didn't. She never looked back.

IX

February 2023

Inspector Devendra Kumar was on his routine patrol when he received a call informing him that his leave application had been approved. The news brought a wave of relief. It was election season, and with the first voting date fast approaching, he had been unsure whether he would be granted time off.

In India, November to March is considered the prime months for weddings, and Inspector Devendra Kumar had planned his daughter's wedding in February almost a year ago. But the announcement of election dates had thrown everything into uncertainty. It had seemed that he might have to miss one of the most important days of his life.

Now, with the confirmation of his leave, he couldn't contain his happiness. He immediately informed his family that he would join them after two days. His family lived in his native city, while he had been posted here for the past three years, a long stay at the same police station and jurisdiction, which was rare. But Devendra Kumar had influential connections among senior officers and politicians. He never hesitated to use those ties when needed, and it had worked in his favour again.

It was February 12, 2023, three days before his leave was set to start. Around noon, after returning to the station, a call came in reporting a dacoity in his area. Without delay, he left for the crime scene with a sub-inspector and two constables. At the victim's house—a plush residence in one of the city's most upscale colonies—Inspector Kumar conducted a thorough inspection.

He spoke to the shaken family, gathering as much detail as possible about the criminals: their clothing, physique, language, any distinguishing traits. He directed forensic experts to collect fingerprints, footprints, and other potential evidence.

The family owned a prominent medical store in the city and was visibly affluent. According to their account, one of the four criminals had posed as an electricity worker to gain entry under the pretext of taking a meter reading. Once inside, he brandished a gun and held the family hostage, allowing his accomplices to enter. They assaulted the head of the family, injuring him severely to instil terror, and then looted gold jewellery, about Rs 50,000 in cash, and other valuables. The involvement of a well-known businessman's family escalated the situation. The city's businessmen's union quickly jumped into the fray. They laid siege to the police lines, raised slogans against the police, and submitted a formal memorandum to the superintendent of police. Their message was clear: if the police failed to solve the case and apprehend the criminals within forty-eight hours, they would launch a full-scale protest against the police and the administration.

Devendra Kumar inwardly cursed the criminals for ruining his plans yet again. Years ago, he had missed his elder son's wedding due to a similar crisis, and now, history was threatening to repeat itself. Returning to the station, Devendra Kumar immediately formed an investigation team and assigned the case to Sub-Inspector Devraj Singh. He instructed Devraj to prioritise the case, ensure daily progress reports, and expedite results.

He was doing everything possible to safeguard his hard-earned leave. But he also knew the risks: a senior officer could intervene at any moment, snatching the case from Devraj's hands and forcing him to take charge personally, especially Circle Officer Dhirendra Singh. Dhirendra Singh, recently promoted, had once competed fiercely with Devendra Kumar for the same post.

Although he won the promotion, old grudges remained, and this could be Dhirendra's opportunity to settle scores.

To pre-empt disaster, Devendra Kumar activated his network of informers, urging them to dig out every scrap of information about the dacoits. He also cleared all pending paperwork and instructed his subordinates to submit all reports before his departure, ensuring no one would have an excuse to disturb him during his leave.

The evening before his leave was to begin, around 7 p.m., he received a phone call. Something about the conversation unsettled him; his face tensed visibly as he listened. Finishing his remaining work quickly, he informed Sub-Inspector Devraj that he was leaving for the day.

Before leaving, he mentioned casually, "I've got a lead in the dacoity case."

Devraj immediately offered to accompany him, but Devendra Kumar declined. "I'll inform you if it's worth pursuing," he said. "If not, I'll proceed to my hometown. Please handle things in my absence and avoid calling me unless it's a real emergency. I'll be back after two weeks. Let me enjoy this leave, I've earned it."

With that, he left, the weight of unfinished business still lingering in the cool night air.

***

The group of businessmen stormed into the office of the superintendent of police, demanding updates on the investigation into the dacoity. Their angry slogans echoed through the station corridors. The SP City, recognising the growing unrest, called the leaders into his office for a discussion. A few press reporters, eager for headlines, accompanied them.

In the meeting, the SP City provided the expected assurances, though internally he knew the reality was far less optimistic. Afterward, the businessmen's union issued a press release, recounting the meeting and highlighting the SP's promise: the criminals would be caught within seventy-two hours.

But in truth, the SP City knew the chances were slim. Immediately after, he rang the Circle Officer (CO) Dhirendra Singh, stressing the urgency of the matter and instructing him to expedite results.

CO Dhirendra Singh saw the situation differently: it was an opportunity to trap Inspector Devendra Kumar. He called Devendra's phone, but it was out of reach. This irritated him even more. He already knew Devendra Kumar was on leave, and he decided to sabotage it. He summoned Sub-Inspector Devraj Singh to his office and demanded a progress report on the dacoity case. As expected, Devraj had nothing concrete.

Seeing his chance, Dhirendra Singh quickly sent a recommendation to cancel Devendra Kumar's leave and issued orders for his immediate return to duty. Approval came swiftly. With a smirk of satisfaction, he tried calling Devendra Kumar again: still unreachable.

Frustrated, Dhirendra Singh ordered Devraj to contact his family and deliver the message. Devraj tried calling Devendra Kumar once more, but nothing. So, he dialled his wife. To his surprise, she revealed that Devendra Kumar hadn't reached home yet. Two days ago, he had called her, saying he needed an extra two days at work before heading home.

Devraj relayed the cancellation order to her, but her anger erupted. "Keep your inspector locked up in your police station! We'll manage by ourselves!" she snapped before hanging up.

Devraj had no choice but to report this to CO Dhirendra Singh, who responded by hurling abuses at Devendra Kumar and insisting Devraj continue trying. The next day, Devraj tried again, but still no connection. By now, serious doubt crept into his mind. This wasn't like Devendra Kumar. It had been three days, but his phone was still unreachable; and he hadn't reached home. Devraj hesitantly called his wife again. This time, she was even angrier and accused the police department of ruining her family's life, especially during her daughter's wedding. When Devraj tried to explain, she refused to listen.

He finally had to raise his voice to stop her, then apologised, calming himself before revealing the truth:

"Madam, Devendra Kumar left the police station four days ago to go home. He had no other official duties. I think... something is wrong."

Panic gripped her. Devraj tried to reassure her, urging her to focus on the wedding, and promised that he would search for Devendra Kumar and, if necessary, involve other officers discreetly.

"Please, madam, stay strong for your daughter," he said gently.

Afterwards, Devraj began a frantic search. He questioned everyone who might know Devendra Kumar's whereabouts, but no one knew anything.

Meanwhile, his responsibilities piled up: managing the police station, being the senior-most officer now; leading the dacoity investigation; and enduring relentless pressure from the businessmen's union.

He reported his fears to CO Dhirendra Singh, suspecting Devendra Kumar might be missing. But Dhirendra Singh dismissed him outright. "He's probably busy with his daughter's wedding," he scoffed.

Adding insult to injury, Dhirendra Singh issued a show-cause notice against Devendra Kumar for dereliction of duty. Everyone in the station knew what was happening—politics—but none dared to speak up.

Devraj continued searching, refusing to give up hope. Then, one morning, the wireless crackled with a grim message: a body had been found on the outskirts of the city.

***

The body was found deep within a farmland thick with a ready crop of golden wheat, waiting to be harvested. A farmer and his wife had come early that morning to begin their work.

It was the wife who noticed it first, faint traces of blood threading through the standing crop.

Curious and worried, she followed the blood trail, her heart pounding harder with every step. Then, she screamed.

The farmer rushed over. What they found froze them in horror: a man's body, slumped on the ground, drenched in blood. Shaking with fear, they immediately called the police helpline. The control room relayed the message to Inspector Vivek Yadav, who rushed to the scene.

But upon arrival, Vivek realised that the farmland was outside his jurisdiction. He quickly notified the control room over the wireless, declaring that the case fell under another police station's area.

The control room then alerted Sub-Inspector Devraj Singh. Devraj reached the farmland to find Vivek Yadav already there, having at least secured the scene by keeping curious villagers away and setting up a perimeter.

However, tension rose quickly, with Vivek Yadav arguing fiercely with Devraj, blaming him for arriving late. A jurisdiction battle broke out between the two police stations. Each officer was eager to avoid taking responsibility for the gruesome discovery.

The argument escalated until Circle Officer Dhirendra Singh arrived. He reviewed the boundary maps and police station records and decided the case would fall under Devraj's station. Devraj attempted to protest, but Dhirendra Singh shut him down firmly, ignoring any counterarguments. Seething inside,

Devraj muttered curses under his breath. He knew exactly why this was happening: he was paying for the sour relationship between Dhirendra Singh and his mentor, Inspector Devendra Kumar.

Still, there was no choice. Devraj steeled himself and proceeded towards the body, joined by Dhirendra Singh and Vivek Yadav. The sight was ghastly. The victim's body was slumped in a seated position, his head bowed. His legs were spread out stiffly, his arms twisted inwards, with wrists resting between his knees.

Blood had soaked into the earth beneath him. Visible on both wrists were deep, angry cuts, clear signs of veins deliberately slashed. Rope marks circled his wrists and ankles, grim reminders of captivity.

Dhirendra Singh carefully lifted one limp arm with a stick, examining the injuries. The wrists bore brutal ligature marks, skin worn raw. His ankles showed the same cruel treatment. Finally, Dhirendra Singh gently raised the victim's blood-caked head.

All three officers recoiled, their hearts lurching in their chests. It was Inspector Devendra Kumar.

For a few long moments, none of them moved. The enmity that Dhirendra Singh had nursed for so long dissolved instantly, replaced by a gnawing guilt that twisted in his gut. He had wanted to trouble Devendra Kumar, humiliate him even, but he had never wished for this.

Now, standing over his lifeless body, he felt the heavy weight of responsibility settle on his shoulders. They began their investigation.

A few metres away, they found a rope tossed carelessly on the ground, stained with blood.

Nearby, droplets of blood led towards the crop. It appeared that Devendra Kumar had been bound, his veins slashed, and then possibly forced or tricked into staggering through the field.

The movement would have accelerated blood loss, hastening death.

While searching the area, the police stumbled upon an abandoned forest department office that had been out of use for a long time. The office was filled with junk, broken tables, and chairs. One room caught the officers' attention due to a new lock on the door. Upon opening it, they found a makeshift hideout. The chairs and tables were arranged in a way that blocked the view from the window. Inside, police discovered food remains, glass, and water bottles.

Forensic experts collected hair samples and took photos of drag marks, but surprisingly, didn't find any fingerprints in the room, not even on the lock. It appeared that the killer had held Devendra Kumar captive in this room for around six to seven days.

It was a slow, torturous end. The officers sealed the crime scene, bagged the evidence, and sent Devendra Kumar's body for a postmortem. Devraj, heartbroken, called Devendra Kumar's family to inform them of the tragedy.

The postmortem report revealed that the killer had tortured Devendra Kumar before taking his life. The completely empty stomach suggested that he had been starved for at least twenty-four hours, underscoring the extreme cruelty and hatred the killer nursed for the man.

The news spread like wildfire throughout the city. A wave of terror swept over the people. Whispers began to circulate: an evil spirit haunted the outskirts. Superstition took hold. People linked this horrific murder to a string of other mysterious deaths in recent years, fuelling tales of an evil tantric or some dark supernatural force at work.

Meanwhile, the police were left grappling with chilling, unanswered questions. What about the phone call that had pulled Devendra Kumar away that evening, the 'lead' he had mentioned in the dacoity case? Was his death connected to the case? Or was this a revenge killing, orchestrated by some old enemy? Or... was there truly something more sinister at play?

The deeper they dug, the darker the mystery seemed to grow.

Ten days had passed. The investigation into both the dacoity and Inspector Devendra Kumar's murder had gone nowhere. The police were empty-handed, fumbling through dead ends and false leads. The pressure from the public, the businessmen's union, and the media mounted with each passing day. Frustration simmered across the city. And then, a spark set everything ablaze.

A news was leaked.

Details of the internal feud between Circle Officer Dhirendra Singh and Inspector Devendra Kumar hit the headlines. Every news channel, every newspaper latched on to the story. In a heartbreaking interview, Devendra Kumar's widow spoke out. Her voice shaking with rage and grief, she squarely blamed CO Dhirendra Singh for her husband's death. She accused him of negligence, claiming that if Dhirendra Singh had taken Sub-Inspector Devraj's concerns seriously, her husband would still be alive. The interview spread like wildfire. The public, already angry, turned outright hostile towards the police administration. The businessmen's union renewed their threats of protests. Public trust plummeted to its lowest.

The pressure on the senior officers became unbearable. They could no longer shield Dhirendra Singh. The first action was swift and decisive: Dhirendra Singh was transferred out of the city.

Officially, it was called an "administrative reshuffle", but everyone knew the truth. Several other station house officers (SHOs) were also transferred. The department needed to show that it was serious about restoring order and credibility. Then came the real change.

A new circle officer was appointed: a young officer, freshly graduated from the State Civil Services Academy. Bright, idealistic, and untainted by internal politics.

The city now found itself under the charge of two young officers, the new CO and a new superintendent of police, both determined to wipe away the stains of the past and clean up the city. Hope began to stir again, quietly, cautiously.

But beneath it all, the darker mystery of Devendra Kumar's death still loomed, unanswered and unresolved. Because whoever had silenced Devendra Kumar was still out there. And they had a head start.

X

April 2023

Devraj Singh reached the new officer's office. He saw her name on the nameplate hanging on the door of her chamber: Kavita Singh. He found Inspector Vivek Yadav wandering in the veranda of the office. Devraj saluted him. Vivek smiled and then whispered, "Madam is not in a good mood. She was in a meeting with Superintendent Sir. She wants results in both cases."

"Have you met her?" Devraj asked him.

"I am waiting, just like you." Vivek smiled again.

"Then how do you know she is not in a good mood?" Devraj asked, a little surprised.

"You must learn to keep these types of information handy when attending a meeting," Vivek advised with a smirk.

Meanwhile, the orderly came to inform them that madam was calling them inside. Kavita Singh was a twenty-eight-year-old unmarried woman. Vivek Yadav, around forty-five years old, had seen many officers in his career, but she was perhaps the youngest of them all.

She smiled upon seeing them and asked if they would like tea or coffee. She instructed the orderly to bring two cups of tea and then started discussing the cases with them. Devraj had no lead in either case. She remained calm for a few minutes. Both Devraj and Vivek Yadav were silently bracing themselves for a harsh reaction.

She thought for a while and then said, "I think, Devraj, you should concentrate on the dacoity case. Yadav ji, you will investigate the Devendra Kumar murder case. We must crack both cases as soon as possible. I will handle the pressure from seniors and politicians, but it is our duty to serve the public."

She assured them of her maximum possible support. When they were leaving, she stopped Devraj and asked him to stay for a minute. Vivek Yadav saluted her and left the room.

She took detailed input on the dacoity case from Devraj and instructed him to update her daily.

Though she spoke gently, the loud and clear message was understood: there was no room for carelessness.

Devraj put in all his efforts to gather any information about the criminals. He stayed in constant contact with his informers. He instructed the beat constables to barricade the roads and check every suspicious person and vehicle.

It was the fortieth day, and he still had no clue or leads in the dacoity case. The CO was supposed to come to his station, and he had no satisfactory answer to her potential questions.

This thought made him tense.

Suddenly, he heard noise outside his office. He came out and saw a woman arguing with a constable. He asked the constable about the matter. The constable abused the woman, calling her a whore, and told Devraj she had come to file a false complaint against a few boys. Devraj scolded the constable for speaking like that and asked the woman to explain her issue. She said that a goon had been troubling her for the last few days. He threatened her, scared her, and sometimes forcefully entered her house. He wanted to have an illicit relationship with her.

The constable interrupted their conversation and said, "Sir, she is a characterless woman. I know her personally. Her husband divorced her."

"He is lying, sir!" the woman shouted. "I filed a divorce from my husband. He used to lynch me for dowry! That goon is his friend. I have seen them consuming alcohol together several times!"

Devraj felt that the woman was lying. He did not want to register one more case unnecessarily, so he told her to settle the matter mutually, and if required, the police would intervene later.

The woman seemed disappointed. She had not expected this attitude from the police. She wanted to say something more, but Devraj asked her to leave and come later. Suddenly, he looked at the gate of the police station. The CO was standing there, silently observing the entire conversation.

Her presence made him speechless. She entered the office and ordered the same constable to bring the woman inside. The constable tried to argue, but Devraj scolded him immediately and ordered him to follow the CO's instruction without question.

The woman came inside the office and repeated the story in front of her. She began to weep when she found sympathy from the CO, Kavita Singh. She listened to her calmly and then instructed Devraj to register her report and take necessary action.

When she left, Kavita said to him, "Devraj ji, I did not expect this attitude from you, and I am not going to tolerate this in the future. You must take it as a warning. Update me in the evening about what action you people take in this matter. I insist you see to this personally. That constable is not reliable."

Devraj wanted to hurl some abusive words, but controlled his desire. Instead, he asked the constable about the man. The constable told him, "He is an informer, sir. Sometimes he misses his relationship with the police. And that woman... she is no saint either. She's a firebrand. Couldn't even manage her marriage for more than a year."

Devraj was already in a sour mood. He instructed the constable to call the man to the police station. In the evening, the constable brought him in and presented him before Devraj. His name was Adil. It was obvious from his body language that he shared a friendly relationship with the constable. Devraj questioned him about the matter concerning the woman. Adil repeated the same story the constable had told Devraj in the morning.

According to Adil, the woman had a loose character. She had married one man, but had an affair with another. Her husband divorced her within a year. Indirectly, he accepted the truth.

He even boasted about how he had caught the woman red-handed with her boyfriend. Adil shamelessly said he had no problem with her or her boyfriend; he simply wanted the same kind of relationship with her.

Suddenly, Devraj slapped him hard. Before Adil could react, another slap landed on his face, numbing him completely. He couldn't utter a single word. Devraj shouted at him,

"What do you think of the police? Who are we? Jokers? If you ever trouble that woman again, I will personally send you to jail!"

The constable quietly took Adil out of Devraj's chamber. Adil was still in shock. He had never expected such behaviour from the police, whom he had always considered his friend. Trying to calm him, the constable offered him tea and said, "Devraj Sir is a good man. It's just... he's disturbed these days because of the dacoity case. Senior officers are pressuring him for results, and he doesn't have a single lead."

Adil, now sitting quietly, spoke in a calm voice, "Investigate Shadab. He might give you some information about the case."

The constable was surprised. "What? What are you saying? Are you sure?" he asked.

Adil didn't say anything more. The constable quickly took Adil back to Devraj and informed him, "Sir, he has information about the dacoity case."

Devraj looked at Adil and asked firmly, "Is this true?"

Adil nodded silently to confirm.

Instantly, Devraj sprang into action. He ordered his staff to prepare for a raid. The address provided was in a densely populated locality, and there was a high possibility of fierce resistance from the locals. He immediately informed the CO about the situation and the potential opposition.

Kavita responded swiftly; she alerted all the nearby police stations and ordered them to fully cooperate with Devraj's team. Within two hours, Shadab was in police custody.

The police gave him the 'best treatment' in the lockup. It took only two slaps to test his tolerance. He opened his mouth immediately.

Shadab was a junk dealer by profession. He usually bought scrap materials, anything that could be sold for a small profit. But the last time, he had bought something that was definitely not junk. He confessed that he had purchased some electronic items, a music system, and a camera from an acquaintance. He paid only a few hundred rupees for them.

The poor man had no idea that his little greed would land him behind bars. In the next ten minutes, he gave Devraj the address and phone number of the person who had sold him the items. Devraj knew there would be no opportunity for sleep or rest now. He immediately raided the given address and picked up the man.

This man was a mediator named Paramjit, also known as Pammi. Pammi made his living by taking commissions in deals like these. He quickly accepted that he had helped to sell the stolen items. He also gave Devraj a new name: the man who was directly in contact with the criminals.

This contact used to inform them whenever he received such consignments. Pammi didn't know much else about him, but he provided a mobile number. Devraj handed it over to the IT cell for tracking.

The number was inactive at that time. Meanwhile, Devraj assigned a team to gather the identification details of the person who had activated it. As expected, the documents were fake. But they managed to trace and pick up the man who had activated the number.

He was a tough nut to crack. Devraj and his men had to work hard to break him down.

But finally, they succeeded. They obtained details of another man, the real handler.

Plain-clothed officers were deployed across all possible locations to trap him.

After three days of continuous tracking, they finally captured him at the bus stand.

Meanwhile, a glitch occurred in the investigation. Mr Batra, the owner of the medical store and the victim of the dacoity, failed to identify the recovered music system and camera as part of the looted material. It was a major setback. But on the other hand, it was a significant success, for they had cracked open an interstate gang of thieves and robbers.

The next day, Devraj was still enjoying the satisfaction of solving an old pending case when he got a call from the CO. She was ready with some papers. She advised him to continue investigating the arrested men. She showed Devraj her calculations and observations and said she had a strong intuition about one of them.

Following her advice, Devraj interrogated the man again, this time more specifically.

This approach worked. The man revealed information about a buyer who had purchased ornaments from the gang. Without losing time, they deployed men to capture the buyer. After two days, they trapped him successfully.

For days, Devraj and his team had faced humiliation for failing to make progress. Now, all that frustration found its outlet. The buyer could not last for more than half an hour under interrogation. He spilt everything.

That night was going to be very eventful. They arrested one of the prime accused at a countryside bar. From him, they gathered information about the other three criminals, who were currently treading the highway, possibly searching for their next target.

It was time for immediate action. CO Kavita Singh quickly formed two teams. She led one herself, and the second was placed under Devraj's supervision. They circulated an urgent message over the wireless. Devraj's team positioned themselves to start chasing the criminals from a turn on the highway, while the CO's team prepared to block their path from the front.

They succeeded in forcing the criminals on to a less crowded road. As per the plan, the CO was ready to intercept them. But the criminals were also alert; they had been observing police movements for the last hour. As soon as they spotted her team, they opened fire.

In reply, her team immediately started counter-firing. At the same time, Devraj and his team reached the spot and joined the firing. The criminals were now trapped.

Suddenly, one man jumped out of the vehicle and ran into the darkness. Kavita noticed it and shouted to attract Devraj's attention. But Devraj was pinned down under heavy firing and couldn't leave his position.

She took a split-second decision and chased the escaping man alone, shouting a challenge and firing a warning shot. The man stopped and raised his hands. She approached him cautiously, keeping her pistol trained on him. Suddenly, he attacked her with brute force. He was heavily built and cruel by nature. He launched a brutal assault, managing to grab and strangle her. She began to choke. Summoning all her strength, she fought back, landing a kick on his private parts, forcing him to bend over. The moment he bent, she kicked him hard on his face.

She quickly recovered her pistol and aimed it at him again. Meanwhile, the police stopped firing on the road. Devraj and his team arrested the other criminals and hurried towards her. He was surprised and impressed to see that the CO had controlled a man much stronger and heavier than her.

The constables quickly arrested him. Devraj asked about the CO's wellbeing. She was panting, but raised her hand to show she was all right.

The next day, the police recovered most of the looted material from various locations. This time, Mr Batra successfully identified his ornaments and other belongings. Devraj finally took a deep sigh of relief. It was a huge success for the police. They had cracked the dacoity case and solved several other robberies.

That evening, CO Kavita Singh held a press conference, proudly declaring the police's success.

At the same time, at a different event, the businessmen's union thanked the police for their prompt action and declared that they would honour the police team.

This success brought great news for Devraj. Senior officers noticed his back-to-back achievements and promoted him. He became the SHO of his police station. He was still basking in the joy of it all when he received a call from the CO. He immediately understood its meaning and, without wasting time, reached her office.

Inspector Vivek Yadav was wandering in the veranda. As usual, Devraj saluted him.

"Inspector Sahib, how are you?" Vivek taunted.

Devraj ignored him and asked, "Has CO Madam arrived at the office?"

"She's an officer. Who dares to question her timing?" It was clear Vivek Yadav was not in a good mood.

They waited there for about fifteen minutes. Then, Kavita Singh arrived. Without delay, she ordered them to follow her into her chamber. She rang the bell and asked the orderly to bring tea for everyone.

Without wasting a minute, she turned to Vivek Yadav and asked, "What is the progress in Inspector Devendra Kumar's murder case?"

Vivek Yadav placed the papers in front of her. She asked for the details. Vivek began explaining everything he had done in the case so far. She listened calmly, and after he finished, she said,

"So, you have no solid lead in this case." She paused for a moment, thinking. Then she turned to Devraj. "Devraj ji, I am assigning this case to you. Please collect all the files from Vivek ji and study them thoroughly."

"Madam, I can handle this case," Vivek Yadav protested, trying to resist her decision.

She replied in a firm but polite tone, "I have more important work for you. Next week, the chief minister of Haryana is visiting to attend a function here. I am assigning you to his escort team. I need an experienced officer to ensure everything goes smoothly."

Vivek couldn't figure out whether the CO was praising him or making a fool out of him.

Sensing his confusion, she added, "Prepare the route plan and security strategy. We'll discuss it tomorrow."

Just then, the orderly arrived with tea. After having their tea, Vivek Yadav asked for permission to leave. She nodded, and he exited the room.

Now alone with Devraj, she discussed the case more seriously. Going through the files, she found several loopholes in Vivek's investigation. Together, they noted down all the missing points and flaws.

She instructed Devraj, "Focus on these weak spots first."

She rang the bell again and asked for another round of tea. While waiting, she casually asked about his family. This question brought a genuine smile to Devraj's face. He began speaking warmly about his wife and two daughters.

The CO listened with interest. She asked more about his daughters, and Devraj's happiness was visible in his body language. Suddenly, she changed the topic. "And what about that lady who came to file a complaint?"

Devraj was caught off guard. He had no immediate answer.

She asked sharply, “Why?”

After a pause, Devraj said, “Madam, that man is an important police informer. We cracked the dacoity case because of his input. We should not lose him.”

She leaned back and thought for a moment. Then she asked, “What are you doing tomorrow morning?”

“Madam, nothing important. Just routine work.”

“Good! I am inviting you for morning tea with my family. Come to my residence at 9 a.m. sharp,” she said.

“Madam...” he tried to say something, but she cut him off with a firm smile.

“I insist.”

The next morning, Devraj arrived at her government bungalow. He informed the orderly, who saluted him and went inside to announce his arrival. After a few minutes, the orderly returned and asked him to come in.

Devraj crossed the garden, entered the house, and was surprised when the CO herself came out to receive him. He felt a little hesitant seeing her personally welcoming him.

At the breakfast table, there were two other people: a woman, and a man around thirty-three years old. Kavita offered him a chair and called the maid to bring breakfast.

She introduced the young man, “This is my elder brother, Rajesh Kumar. He’s an IAS officer, posted in Kanpur.”

Hearing this, Devraj immediately stood up and saluted. Rajesh smiled and nodded, gesturing to him to sit down. Just then, another man, around thirty-eight years old, appeared from another room. Kavita and Rajesh stood up to show their respects.

She introduced him too. "This is my eldest brother. He's an electrician by profession. He has his own shop in our native town."

She carefully watched Devraj's facial expressions while saying this.

Meanwhile, the eldest brother asked teasingly, "Pinki, what's for breakfast today?"

She laughed and replied, "Brother, it's your favourite dish!"

After breakfast, she asked Devraj with a serious expression, "Did you notice anything unusual about my family?"

Devraj thought for a moment and answered, "All of you are unmarried."

"Correct!" she said. "Do you want to know why?"

He stayed silent, not knowing what to say. She took his silence as eagerness and continued, "It is because of an irresponsible police officer. When I was a child, a goon assaulted me, and a corrupt, insensitive officer protected him. We were forced to leave our city, our roots, our everything."

Devraj listened, speechless. Now he understood why she had invited him for breakfast. She concluded with strong emotions in her voice, "Devraj ji, I have a good impression of you. I respect your sincerity. But I will never tolerate any crime against women. I can sacrifice everything to protect even a single woman."

"Madam, I understand your concern, but this man is an important informer," Devraj tried to explain respectfully.

She looked at him steadily for a moment and then said firmly, "Okay. Continue using him, but make sure that woman is not troubled again. Your informer should stay away from her. Understood?"

Devraj nodded, absorbing her clear instructions. He stood up, saluted her, and said sincerely,

"Thank you, madam... not just for the breakfast, but for the honour and trust you have shown in me."

She smiled briefly, and Devraj left her residence. At the police station, his constable was waiting outside his office with Adil, the informer. The constable greeted Devraj with a salute and said, smiling, "Sir, Adil truly deserves a reward. His information was spot on."

Without saying much, Devraj handed an envelope to Adil, a small reward for his cooperation. Adil accepted it with a broad smile and turned to leave. But before he could exit, Devraj stopped him. His voice turned serious, "Adil, listen carefully. Improve your behaviour. I will not save you the next time if you cross the line again, especially with any woman. Stay away from that lady. Do not even try to approach her again."

Adil lowered his eyes, sensing the change in his tone. As he turned to leave, Devraj gave him one last warning, "I will personally keep an eye on this matter. If you trouble her even once, you will find me standing against you."

Adil nodded silently and hurried out of the station, sensing that this time, Devraj meant every single word.

XI

March 1997

The breakup broke Shirish. He lost interest in everything, forgot how to smile, and lost the joy of life. He always remained in a bad mood. It affected his studies, as he could not concentrate.

Soon, his father noticed it. One day, while going for a walk, he asked Shirish to accompany him. He was not interested in going, but could not deny his father's request. They took a long walk and reached a sewer. His father showed him the sewer and asked him about it.

Shirish did not understand what his father wanted to know. His father simplified the question for him. "Okay! Tell me five special things about this."

Still, Shirish did not understand, but he had to answer. So, he said, "It cleans the garbage of the city."

"Anything else?" his father asked.

Shirish thought hard but could not find anything else to say. His father smiled and said, "Look carefully, there are many places in this sewer where the litter clogs up, obstructing the water, but it cannot stop its flow. Water finds its way. Similarly, life should not stop for any reason. It must flow. Leave all bad memories behind like that litter. If a sewer can do it, why can't you?"

At that moment, he understood why his father had brought him there. He bowed his head. His father patted his back and tried to raise his courage. It helped him. He felt his heart become lighter, like a feather. They returned home, and that night they played chess till late. It was their favourite pastime. Shirish decided to forget everything, and started afresh immediately.

Several months passed since Shirish's second heartbreak. The pain did not fade entirely, but life, with its quiet indifference, continued. He stopped looking at girls with interest, convinced that love wasn't meant for him. The scars from his failed relationships had left him questioning his worth, and the very idea of someone accepting him seemed far-fetched now.

As summer approached, slowly and drowsily, he found himself at a crossroads. It had been a year since he completed his graduation, and his family's financial situation hadn't allowed him to pursue further education. For months, he had been job-hunting, taking on tutoring to make ends meet. His father was unwell, adding to his responsibilities. His focus was solely on supporting his family, but one day, something shifted, setting the stage for a significant change in his life.

One morning, while sipping tea at his door, he happened to see Mini getting ready for college. It wasn't the first time he was seeing her, but something was different that day, maybe the light, maybe his mood, or maybe just her smile. She looked radiant, like a rose in full bloom, and he found himself staring longer than he intended to.

She noticed. Their eyes met, and Shirish quickly looked away, embarrassed. She went back inside, but her image lingered in his mind. He tried to study that day, but every page reminded him of her face. He told himself it was just a passing distraction, nothing more.

But it wasn't.

In the evening, while pacing on the roof, he caught sight of her walking to her tuition class. He remained there, pretending to enjoy the breeze, but the truth was undeniable: his eyes were waiting for her.

A strange pull began to form. Perhaps it wasn't just Mini's beauty, but the simplicity, calmness, and familiarity she carried. She wasn't a stranger. She was the girl next door, part of the world he had always known, but had never noticed in this way. Maybe, after all the emotional wreckage he'd been through, it was this sense of closeness and safety that made his heart drift towards her.

He knew the hesitation within himself. The fear of failure, of rejection, still haunted him. His past had made him doubt whether he was worth being loved at all. And yet, every time he saw Mini, something inside him softened.

Soon, his behaviour began to change. He stood at his gate when she left for college. In the evenings, he found himself waiting on the roof, watching her leave for tuition, and staying there until she returned, without even realising why. The heart, once again, had begun to disobey him.

One day, something unusual happened. His sister, who was a friend of Mini, told him something that scared him. She said that a boy from the colony had proposed to Mini by sending her a love letter. Mini was angry at his daring and went to his family to complain about his rudeness. The boy had to apologise for his deed, and he promised to never follow or trouble her again. His family was also ashamed of his act. This incident made Mini famous in society as a brave girl.

Shirish did not want the same thing to happen to him. So, he learnt a lesson from this episode and tried to suppress his feelings. This was a time when the main topic of Hindi films was love and love stories. He did his best to extinguish the fire of his emotions, but somewhere, a spark remained.

A few days passed, and he was busy memorising his notes for an upcoming government job examination when he saw her on the roof. She looked puzzled; perhaps she was waiting for someone. It distracted him from his studies. He kept a watch on her.

Nobody was in the street. A curiosity arose in his mind: whom was she waiting for?

Suddenly, a boy appeared from the far side of the road. Mini stood at the same corner of the roof. Shirish's doubt hardened into certainty; she was waiting for that boy. His heart sank under the weight of disappointment. Twice he had failed in love, and now this boy was taking Mini from him. A silent fear gripped him, the fear of losing her without ever confessing his feelings.

When the boy approached Mini's house, she moved to that corner of the roof. Convinced she was waiting for him, Shirish prepared to catch them red-handed, desperate to confirm his worst fear. Suddenly, a girl appeared from another street, passing by Mini's house. He knew her well; she was Mini's friend.

She screamed when she saw Mini, "Idiot! Come fast! I have been waiting for you for the last thirty minutes."

"I searched this book with difficulty. You had dropped it behind the almirah," Mini replied.

Meanwhile, the boy passed by her house, and Mini did not pay any heed to him. She was busy talking to her friend. He felt immense relief; his doubt was baseless. At that moment, he realised he was truly in love with her.

He sat down in deep thought, but his heart was not ready to follow his mind, which suggested he stay away from her. Once he accepted that he was in love, the spark he had been trying to suppress became a flame. His determination began to burn in those flames.

That evening, while he was teaching Animesh, Mini approached him. She had a problem in English and needed his help. Shirish took the book and solved her query. It was a simple problem, and Mini was known to be an intelligent girl. Even while explaining it, he felt that she already knew the solution. It made him excited. He felt that Mini wanted to talk to him and had used this as a reason.

He firmly believed in his assumption. To clarify the matter, he decided to write a letter to her. The morning he was about to throw the letter in front of her house, he saw the boy who had dared to do the same previously. It shocked him. His faith shattered at that moment. He did not want the same incident to happen to him. He immediately withdrew his plan.

The way he had solved Mini's problem in English had impressed her. Shirish took an interest in cricket, and Mini was a blind fan of the Indian cricket team. It opened a channel of conversation between them.

He used to tutor Animesh last among all his students, around 8 p.m. He taught him for one hour and then discussed the performance of the Indian cricket team with the two siblings.

Mini and Animesh's parents were friendly with him. Sometimes, they also joined the discussions. It was the best time of Shirish's life. Talking with Mini increased his energy level.

His days became golden, and his nights turned silvery. He still did not dare to express his feelings to Mini, but it did not matter. He was happy just to spend time with her.

A year passed. Animesh was promoted to the next class. That's when the first shock came: Animesh had decided to join his class teacher's tuitions. It meant discontinuing Shirish's tutoring. It also meant that the daily meetings between Shirish and Mini would stop. Still, he maintained good relations with Mini's family. He often visited their home. Sometimes, he got the opportunity to talk to her.

On one occasion, Shirish was watching a cricket match on the TV at Mini's house. Mini and he were alone in the room. They talked and discussed about cricket for hours until her mother became angry at her.

It was perhaps the last time he watched a cricket match at her house. However, he used to go to her home on a few occasions. One day, Mini's mother called him. Any invitation to her house made him happy. So, he visited them in the evening. It was his calculated time; he could spend more time with Mini.

He reached and started talking to Mini and Animesh. Her mother came into the room and gave him a bag. He did not understand what to do with it. The bag contained some used clothes and shoes of Animesh, Mini, and their sister. Her mother was offering these clothes to him and his brother and sister.

He refused to accept them because it hurt his ego and self-respect. Mini's mother insisted he take the bag with him, but he refused. He returned home with a wounded ego. That day, he understood the difference in economic status between Mini's family and his own.

After this incident, he did not go to their house again, but it was difficult for him to forget her. He realised that Mini was not within his reach. So, he decided not to show his emotions to her.

It was not an easy task. He tried to divert his attention to other activities.

He shut the door that opened towards her house. He did not go to the roof at the time she left for her tuition.

One evening, he peeped outside from the window. He saw Mini standing on the roof. She smiled when she saw him, and all his determination evaporated. He could not stop himself from smiling back.

That evening, he opened all the doors. It was the beginning of a new chapter in his life. He decided not to stop himself from loving her.

He kept a watch on her. He enjoyed listening to the sound of her footsteps and could easily recognise them. He would wait the whole evening just to catch a glimpse of her, to hear the sound of her steps.

One day, it became too much. It irritated her. She patted her forehead in anger when she saw him at the door. It demoralised him. He had thought that she understood his feelings, but this act told him that she did not like him, that his presence irritated her. He decided not to trouble her again.

This time, he shut the window too. Twice or thrice, his mother scolded him for this. When she opened the door, he sat behind the wall so that no one could see him. He stopped going to the roof. He took special care while commuting between home and college, to avoid being visible to her. At the same time, his interaction with Animesh also reduced. Animesh was growing into a teenager and had his own circle of friends.

Ten days passed. It was proving difficult for him to continue the same routine. Many times, he heard and recognised the sound of her footsteps. This sound acted like a cardio accelerator because he had no control over his ears or his heartbeat.

He did not need his eyes to see her; his ears and his heart told him where she was, which corner of her home she was in.

It was a Sunday in June. The weather was pleasant, and he forgot the routine he had followed for the last ten days. He opened the door and was enjoying the breeze when suddenly, she opened her door and saw him. She immediately shut it. It was very disappointing for him. He cursed his foolishness. He had ruined the discipline he had maintained for ten days.

He wanted to close the door, but suddenly, she opened the door again and came to the gate. She looked at him for a moment and then started enjoying the weather. He could not fathom whether he should shut the door or keep standing there. He could not shut the door. Mini stood there for more than thirty minutes. Then her mother called her, and before going inside, she looked at him for a moment. He could not believe what had happened. He lingered there for another fifteen minutes, hoping that she might come again.

Once again, the same routine started, until she showed her anger the same way. This on-and-off dynamic continued for the next six months.

The annual festival of Holi arrived, the festival of colours, fun, and joy.

A group of boys danced at the crossing. Shirish picked a spot from where he would be visible to her. He displayed his dancing skills. He thought he had made his best effort to impress her.

During his dance, he kept glancing at her window. He wanted to confirm whether she was watching him or not. He was happy and satisfied with his performance.

The next day of the festival when he was standing on the street, a cloth from her roof drifted in the breeze and dropped somewhere on the road. Mini and her mother were on the roof. Her mother asked him to find the fabric. He searched here and there but could not find it.

Mini tried to show him where it was, but he failed to notice it. Finally, she had to call him, "Brother! It is there."

It felt like someone had poured boiling water into his ears. He did not want to be Mini's brother. He picked up the cloth and gave it to her mother. His excitement faded, and only a bad mood remained. He spent the whole day feeling upset.

At night, he thought about it. What wrong had she done? She could not have addressed him differently in her mother's presence. This thought gave him immense relief. Suddenly, his mood lifted.

One more year passed. He was still unsure whether Mini had any feelings for him or not. The on-and-off relationship did not allow him to believe in it. In this relation, he was only sure of one thing: his mad, deep love for her. He knew he could never feel the same way for anyone else in his life. It had become a divine feeling for him.

Mini was not just a girl for him; she had become the symbol of love itself. He firmly believed that he would get a job one day, and then he would ask her parents for permission to marry her.

***

It was Mini's younger sister's birthday. They had invited all her friends, but not Shirish's sister, who he thought was her friend. It was not an uncommon thing because most of the guests were her college friends.

At night, Mini's mother knocked on the door of Shirish's house. His mother opened the door.

She offered her the leftover food from the party.

Their family was poor in terms of money. They were suffering from an economic crisis, and sometimes they had to skip meals because they had nothing to eat, but they had self-respect. This offer hurt their self-respect and ego deeply.

This time, all his beliefs shattered. He understood that Mini's parents would never permit her to marry him. He knew Mini well, and knew she would never go against her family. It was like a massive hammer had hit his feelings.

By this time, he was deeply in love with her. He had done whatever he could to have her in his life. He had been to temples and all possible places of worship to please God. Perhaps God was not happy with him.

Then, one day, he faced the most challenging moment of his life: his father passed away after suffering from cancer for many years. It was the biggest shock for the family. They had to shift to a different locality.

He had to leave behind the only thing still in his control: the ability to watch her from afar. The bad times did not end there; they continued. One day, he got a chance to visit his old home.

He grabbed this opportunity with both hands. He reached the house of his ex-landlord and completed the work for which he had come.

While he was there, he noticed that Animesh and his friends were running here and there, looking busy and excited. He asked the landlord's daughter what was happening. She told him that it was Mini's engagement ceremony.

Shirish had no words; he did not know how to react. It was the end of all hopes, all votive offerings, and all feelings. The brightness of the day suddenly turned into darkness. He fell numb and speechless.

XII

May 2023

Devraj sat across from the CO, who was reviewing a set of files on her table, carefully going through each one. After a moment of silence, she looked up and asked, "So, what have you concluded from your investigation so far?"

"Madam, I came across another case that happened in this area, which bears striking similarities to the one we're investigating," Devraj replied.

"Which case are you referring to?" she enquired, her curiosity piqued.

"The Dr Prakash murder case," Devraj answered.

"Where was the victim's body found? Was it under the same police station's jurisdiction?" she asked, her voice sharp.

"No, madam. It was under a different police station."

"What was the exact location?" she pressed further, leaning slightly forward.

"It was under the Shahabad police station's jurisdiction, right here," he said, pointing to a spot on the map.

She studied the map, her finger tracing the lines of jurisdiction. "Have you noticed something interesting?" she asked, glancing up at him. "This location is right on the border of the jurisdiction. Inspector Devendra Kumar's body was found in nearly the same situation. I've heard rumours about a jurisdiction dispute."

"Yes, madam! Technically, it was under Vivek Yadav's jurisdiction, but CO Dhirendra Singh had a personal conflict with Devendra Kumar. So, he assigned the case to his own station," Devraj chuckled lightly.

"But it was the murder of Devendra Kumar!" she said, raising an eyebrow in disbelief.

"Madam, who actually bothered to check the body? Dhirendra Kumar wanted to send a message, and Vivek Yadav wasn't eager to take on a case that could bring him more trouble," Devraj laughed, a touch of cynicism in his voice.

"Strange," she murmured thoughtfully. "If the killer in both cases is the same, then one thing is clear: this person knows the jurisdictions inside out." She paused for a moment, her mind clearly working through the details. "Devraj, can you arrange the photos of Dr Prakash? It might help us find a connection between these two murders. And send a query to all the nearby police stations. We need to know if there have been any similar cases."

"Understood, madam," Devraj replied, standing up and saluting her.

***

Devraj had gathered all the information and photos CO Kavita Singh had requested. He visited both crime scenes, spoke with local people, and collected as much detail as he could about the cases. After thoroughly analysing the information, he drew some conclusions. However, before proceeding further, he wanted to show his findings to her. He realised he had become a fan of the CO's working style, and he had developed a strong desire for her appreciation.

The CO was on leave for fifteen days. It was a joyous occasion for her family as they had found a bride for their eldest brother. Devraj knew that her family had been eagerly waiting for this moment for a long time. He didn't want to disturb her during this time, so he continued his investigation on his own.

After a fortnight, when she returned to duty, Devraj met her with his files. She greeted him with a warm smile and asked about his progress. He opened the files and began explaining his findings. But before he could go further, she stopped him and motioned for him to sit. She offered him sweets.

"Thank you, madam," he said, and then resumed his explanation, going over the details he had collected and his conclusions. He showed her the photos of both victims and pointed out the locations of the crimes, which were only about five kilometres apart.

He detailed the similarities between the cases: both victims were government officials, both were involved in crime investigations, and both had been murdered in almost identical ways. The bodies of both victims had been discovered in a similar pattern. Most importantly, the time of death in both cases was remarkably close, between 2 and 5 a.m.

Based on these similarities, Devraj concluded that the same killer was responsible for both murders. The CO appeared impressed by his thorough work. After a brief pause, she said, "You've done impressive work. Now, we're certain of one thing: the killer in these cases is the same."

"Thank you, madam!" he said, pleased with her praise.

"Devraj ji, this is not the end of the investigation. The real work begins now. There's much more to be done, but I'm certain of one thing: I made no mistake assigning this case to you," she said, her tone confident.

"Yes, madam!" Devraj accepted her challenge, eager to continue.

"We still have a few more questions to answer," she said, writing them down on a piece of paper. "First, is this the work of a serial killer? Second, what could be the killer's motive? Third, is someone trying to mislead us with the serial killer theory? Fourth, and most importantly, are these the only two cases, or has he killed more people?"

"Madam, I believe finding the answer to the fourth question is crucial. It will likely help us answer the other three," he replied, snapping a photo of the paper with her queries.

"We have to solve this, Devraj ji, and we need to stop him before he kills again," she said with determination.

"Madam, I will put in my best effort to crack this case," he said, standing up and saluting her.

"I know, Devraj ji. You're the best officer to solve this case. My best wishes are with you, and please keep me updated on your progress," she said, her trust in him evident.

***

Devraj had asked for details from all the nearby police stations, but he hadn't received a response from any of them. Realising that the answers wouldn't come quickly, and not wanting to wait, he decided to visit the crime scene again.

The place had changed completely. The bushes had become denser. Devraj's hope of finding something useful began to fade as he found himself inspecting the area without any clear direction. He spent half an hour thoroughly examining everything, but as expected, he found nothing.

Some villagers saw him and gathered around his car. Feeling thirsty, he asked them for some water. In India, the police are often seen as an unfamiliar presence in rural areas, so the villagers were a bit nervous. One man quickly ran off and brought him water. Devraj started a conversation about the murders, and the villagers were eager to share their thoughts. One of them said, "Sir, it's the work of a ghost. No man can do this."

All his companions laughed at him. Devraj smiled too, but the man, clearly embarrassed, repeated his statement, "Believe me, sir, haven't you seen? All the dead men were strong and well built. How could a single person overpower them? Even two or three men couldn't control them."

"All the men who died? But... there was only one man!" Devraj corrected him.

"No, sir! Three men have been found dead around this area," one of the villagers interrupted. "One here, one in Ursala village, and one in Shahabad."

"Ursala? When did that happen?" Devraj asked, surprised.

"I think it was about three and a half years ago," the villager replied after thinking for a moment.

That was important information. Devraj immediately went to the police station that covered Ursala village to enquire about any similar cases. It took two days for the details to arrive, and when Devraj opened the case file, he was shocked by what he found.

The victim's name was Vijay, a notorious figure involved in a highly publicised blackmailing case. Devraj knew all the details of the case, but it was a shock to find out that Vijay was also one of the victims of the so-called serial killer.

Once again, Devraj found himself at a cul-de-sac. He had managed to establish a connection between the murders of Dr Prakash and Inspector Devendra Kumar, both government officials involved in criminal investigations. However, he could not link the murder of Vijay to the same pattern. Vijay had been killed nearly one and a half years earlier, and the circumstances seemed different.

Devraj shared his findings with the CO. He was caught in a dilemma: was the murderer selecting victims randomly, or was there a specific set of targets? He discussed his doubts with her, but even she could not form a perfect theory to connect the murders.

Devraj, however, had a strong instinct that the murderer was not choosing victims at random. He believed the killer had a specific list, and that more murders could be imminent. He voiced his concerns to the CO, who recognised the seriousness of his fears and decided to take the matter seriously.

He also told her about the villagers' beliefs regarding the murders. She laughed off their theory about a ghost being responsible, but Devraj urged her to focus on the physical characteristics of the victims. After thinking for a while, she asked, "So, you're suggesting that there might be more than one murderer?"

"No, madam. I'm sure there's only one murderer," he replied confidently.

"And why are you so certain?"

"Madam, Dr Prakash lived a simple life and had no known personal enemies. His murder had to have a specific reason. The same applies to Inspector Devendra Kumar. Although he had connections with senior officers and some politicians, if a group were behind the murders, there would likely have been an internal conflict about choosing such a high-profile target. But here, there's no mess, no mistakes, just a repetition of the same pattern."

He showed her photos of the victims' wounds. "Even if you examine the fatal wounds, you'll notice a pattern," he explained. "Vijay's hands had three to four cuts, and his thigh had more than five simple but severe cuts. In Dr Prakash's case, the number of wounds was drastically less, just two cuts on his hands and two on his thighs. And in Inspector Devendra Kumar's case, the incisions were even more precise. The killer learnt how to slash the veins more efficiently with each murder."

Kavita admitted that Devraj's reasoning was solid. They still didn't have much information about the criminal, but they knew a few things: he had a muscular physique and was likely skilled in martial arts. Beyond that, they had no concrete leads.

They didn't have to wait long for the next development. The police received a report of another victim who had been found dead in the same manner. As expected, this body was discovered in a different jurisdiction. The area was on the outskirts of the city, and within a two-kilometre radius, the boundaries of four different police stations intersected. The killer appeared to be exploiting his knowledge to mislead the police.

When the message came through on the wireless, the CO immediately realised that it was the same killer. She informed Devraj and instructed him to head to the crime scene. Once again, the murder mirrored the previous ones.

This time, however, Kavita and Devraj were prepared. They had already identified the killer's method and anticipated the trick. She quickly instructed the SHO of the police station where the body had been found to circulate the victim's details among all the nearby police stations. She was confident that the victim's missing person's report must have been filed at one of the stations. She asked the SHO to get the victim's identification as soon as possible and to keep both Devraj and her in the loop.

Her instincts were right. Devraj found the missing person's report at the city police station. The victim's wife identified the body. The man's name was Nitin, a twenty-five-year-old businessman who had recently taken over his father's import-export company dealing in medicines.

Devraj didn't have to work hard to find the connection between Nitin and Vijay. Their fathers were relatives, and the two of them had been childhood friends. A few years ago, they had even gone to Bangkok together for a trip, which highlighted the strong bond they shared.

Now, Devraj had two pairs of victims. Each pair had a connection, Dr Prakash and Inspector Devendra Kumar were both government officials involved in criminal investigations, while Vijay and Nitin were linked by family ties and their shared history. But there was no obvious connection between the two pairs, except for one possible factor: a common killer.

Devraj's instincts told him there was a deeper link connecting the four victims, that this link was just within his reach, but he couldn't quite see it. Something was missing, and he was determined to find it, no matter how elusive it seemed.

XIII

June 2013

Shirish was working as an executive in an FMCG company. That year, he received a promotion to area sales manager, which came with a salary increase and an elevated status within the company.

To celebrate this success and thank God, Shirish and his family decided to go on a pilgrimage to Kedarnath, a famous Hindu site in the Garhwal Himalayas near the Mandakini River. They were joined by his sister's family, her husband, and three of his friends. The trek to the main temple is one of the most challenging in India.

After a two-day journey by car, they reached Gauri Kund, the base camp for the trek, at around 6 p.m. They had previously trekked to Vaishno Devi in Kashmir, where pilgrims travelled day and night to reach the temple. They had assumed the Kedarnath trek would be similar. However, they were wrong. As they began their ascent, darkness quickly engulfed the entire hill. That evening, the power supply was interrupted in the area, and for the first time, they experienced a profound, almost suffocating darkness. The temperature, which was 46°C in the plains, had dropped to around 2–3°C in the hills.

Despite the cold, they continued for almost three kilometres. Soon, the temperature dropped further, and the biting cold air seemed to pierce their bones. Realising they couldn't continue at night, they tried to find shelter, but there were no places available. They asked an experienced fellow traveller, who suggested staying at one of the stalls along the way. Initially, they thought he was joking, but when the milestone revealed that Rambara was still eleven kilometres away, they decided to seek refuge at one.

One stall was about to shut for the night. The owner agreed to let them stay for Rs 200 per person, with the condition that they vacate by 6 a.m. They reluctantly agreed. Shirish couldn't help but curse the owner when they paid Rs 1600 for the night, but once inside, the warmth of the quilts made it worth every penny. They slept soundly, their best rest in a long time.

The stall owner woke them up early in the morning. He had made arrangements, including a temporary washroom, for their convenience. After a quick freshen-up, they decided to hire ponies for the rest of the journey, but Shirish chose to trek on foot. He wanted to experience the natural beauty of the place and capture it on his newly bought smartphone.

As Shirish was about to leave, he noticed a familiar face among the group of ponies. He couldn't recognise her at first, but then it struck him. It was Mini. She was there with her family: her husband, mother-in-law, daughters, and sister-in-law. All of them had ponies, although it seemed Mini was reluctant to ride hers.

Shirish pointed her out to his family. His younger brother and sister excitedly called out to her, and she smiled when she saw them. His sister went to meet her, and after a brief formal introduction of the two families, her family decided to continue the journey. Mini's husband encouraged her to ride the pony, but she was hesitant, her fear evident in her expression.

Her husband grew frustrated, believing she was throwing a tantrum. He shouted at her, which only embarrassed her, and tears welled up in her eyes. The tension seemed to escalate until Shirish intervened. He offered, "Sir, I'm walking to the temple. If Mini wants, she can join me."

Mini looked at him and nodded. Her husband, clearly relieved, indicated the meeting point where he would expect her to join him, and ordered the rest of the group to move on.

As the muleteer was about to leave with the group, Shirish noticed the man's disappointed expression. He handed him Rs 200 to thank him for his services. His face lit up, and he blessed Shirish before moving off in search of another customer.

Shirish felt a sense of gratitude towards the man, but more importantly, he felt as if God had given him another reason to journey to Kedarnath: Mini was now walking beside him.

Before they left the area, Shirish couldn't help but steal a glance at her. She hadn't changed much in appearance, and still had the same physique and way of dressing. But for a moment, he felt like time had reversed. He remembered the days when he used to stand on his roof or stare at her from behind his window.

She caught him staring and teased, "If you're done staring, let's move!"

Shirish felt embarrassed, and they started walking together. He was much taller and had longer strides, so he quickly pulled ahead, leaving Mini behind by about fifty metres.

"Shirish!" she called out. Surprised, he turned to see her struggling to keep up. He stopped and waited for her. She came closer and, with a playful tone, said, "You still have the habit of leaving me behind."

Shirish couldn't decide whether it was a playful remark or a sarcastic jab. He wasn't sure how to respond, but decided to match her pace. Suddenly, she stumbled and almost lost her balance. Without thinking, Shirish offered her his hand to help steady herself. His heart raced as he braced himself for rejection. He feared he had made a mistake and ruined the little progress he had made with her. He squeezed his eyes shut and crossed his fingers. Then, he felt her soft, warm hand in his palm.

When he looked at her, she deliberately avoided eye contact. But for Shirish, it felt like a moment of connection, a fleeting moment that gave him hope.

Shirish tightened his grip around her fingers, and she responded in kind. His anxiety slowly melted away, and his heartbeat gradually returned to normal. They walked together in comfortable silence for a while, until, unexpectedly, Shirish stumbled. This time, it was Mini who steadied him.

That day, for Shirish, became the most beautiful day of his life. He couldn't contain his thoughts any longer and asked, "May I ask you something?"

"You can ask me anything," she replied with a warm smile.

Her words made him hesitate. Mini sensed his uncertainty and encouraged him gently, "Please, ask! You might not get this opportunity again, and I might not have the chance to answer you."

Shirish gathered his courage and asked, "Why did you say that?"

Mini looked at him, her smile never fading. "What did I say?"

"A few minutes ago, you said something about my habit of leaving you behind," he murmured.

She looked him in the eye, her gaze steady. "Because you do leave me behind."

"Was that all?" he asked.

"Do you think there was another meaning?" she teased, a playful glint in her eyes.

Shirish, caught off guard, didn't answer. To avoid the tension, he resumed walking. Mini smiled and matched his pace, though she soon showed signs of exhaustion. "Let's take a break," she suggested.

They stopped, and Shirish bought a bottle of water for her. Looking at his watch, he noted, "It's around 10 a.m. If we don't reach the temple by 1.30 p.m., it'll close for the next three hours."

Mini, however, responded with an unexpected question, "Is my company so boring that you want to get rid of me?"

Shirish felt his heart skip a beat, but he quickly replied, "I would like to accompany you... till eternity." It wasn't something he had planned to say, but it slipped out, leaving him slightly embarrassed.

"Oh, is that why you've been leaving me behind every time?" she replied quickly.

He smiled. "So, the sentence had a different meaning too."

"You take a long time to understand things," she remarked in a dull voice.

"I knew it," he said with a faint grin.

"But you didn't take the pain to express it," she complained.

"The timing wasn't in my favour to express anything," he explained, looking slightly apologetic.

"Timing." She laughed sarcastically, and Shirish could tell it was a jab at his past hesitations.

Suddenly, he asked, "Did you ever love me?"

"No, I never loved you. That's why I'm accompanying you now," she said, her tone somewhat playful.

Shirish pressed on, "Please, answer me. It's a question of my life and faith."

Mini's face grew more serious. "That time has passed. Why are you still clinging to it? You'll find nothing."

"That's not an answer," he said firmly, his frustration mounting.

"What will you get from my answer? It won't change anything. Please don't ask me this," she said, turning to walk ahead.

Shirish, feeling helpless, could only follow her. Mini paused, looking back at him. "Come on, we need to reach the temple before 1.30 p.m."

His steps grew heavier, as though he didn't want to reach the end of this journey. But Mini understood his mood. Suddenly, she spoke up, "You haven't taken any photos of me. I know I'm not as beautiful as this valley, but I at least deserve one picture, don't I?"

A smile broke out on Shirish's face as he pulled out his phone and began clicking pictures of her. After taking three or four, she extended her hand towards him. At first, Shirish thought she wanted him to hold her hand, but instead, she pointed at his phone.

"Do you want a photo with me? Give your phone to someone to take the picture," she suggested.

Shirish handed his phone to a passerby, who agreed to take their photo. They stood side by side for the shot, but the man asked them to move closer. Shirish, surprised, moved towards Mini. Then, unexpectedly, she took his arm and wrapped it around her tightly.

It felt like a once-in-a-lifetime experience for Shirish. The warmth of her body against his was overwhelming. She playfully tickled his nose, teasing, "How's your mood? Happy?"

Shirish smiled but couldn't find the right words. Mini grinned again and added, "See, time never returns. So, enjoy it while it lasts, like I am."

It was as if everything had changed. Where before, they had walked in silence, now she was vocal and full of energy. She was clearly enjoying every moment of the journey.

Suddenly, she spotted a flower growing in the valley below and squealed with childlike excitement. "Look at that flower! It's beautiful!" she exclaimed, pointing to the blossom.

Shirish took out his phone and snapped a picture of it.

"Can you pluck it for me?" she asked eagerly.

He looked at her in surprise. "Are you sure? It's way down in the valley."

"Yes, I'm sure. Please, can you bring it for me?" she insisted.

Shirish hesitated, but then, gathering all his courage, he began to make his way down towards the flower. As he descended, he felt an unexpected weightlessness and almost lost his footing. He had to run down the slope, using sheer instinct to maintain his balance. Thankfully, he found a tree trunk to hold on to, stabilising himself. He crawled down carefully and reached the flower.

After plucking it, he handed it to her. She took it with a grin, tucking it inside her bag. Then she looked at him and asked, "Tell me the truth, you felt the thrill, didn't you?"

"Thrill? I'm just thankful I'm still alive," he replied, making her laugh.

They were now just three kilometres away from the temple, and the path had levelled out. The temple was now visible in the distance. Shirish realised that this beautiful moment, this dreamlike day, was nearing its end. He decided to stop at a tea stall and offer her a break.

They sat down, and he ordered two cups of tea and a packet of biscuits.

It was the final, peaceful moment before they reached their destination.

While sipping tea, Shirish asked about Mini's family. She smiled, her eyes lighting up as she began to speak. She spoke about her two beautiful daughters: the elder was studying in class four; the younger, in class one. Her husband, she said with pride, was a state-level wrestler and an officer at the Food Corporation of India. Her words painted a picture of a happy family, and her expressions told the rest of the story, a life of contentment and fulfilment.

Shirish didn't know how to react. His emotions tangled inside him, a strange blend of happiness for her and sadness for himself. Perhaps Mini noticed the struggle in his eyes, because she said softly, "I am happy. I am satisfied with my life. No one gets everything they desire in life. Some aches remain... It's the story of life."

Shirish stayed silent. The ache inside him deepened. Mini then asked about his life. He only smiled a sarcastic, hollow smile. She insisted, urging him to share.

He finally spoke, "There's nothing special about my life. After your marriage, I lost interest in everything. But... life doesn't stop. I had to survive, had to support my family. So, I joined an FMCG company as a sales executive. It gave me enough to fulfil my responsibilities. Five years ago, I got my sister married, and that's pretty much the whole story."

Mini watched him carefully, then asked, "Why did you lose interest in life after my marriage?"

He looked away, trying to avoid her gaze.

"Tell me... why?" she pressed again.

"You know why," he muttered.

"No, I don't," she said, her voice steady but serious.

Shirish felt exposed, the same helplessness he had once felt when she had caught him staring years ago. "Let's leave this topic," he whispered.

"No! You have to tell me." She was firm, waiting, but he remained silent.

After a long pause, Mini spoke, her voice low but clear, "Fine. Then let me tell you something instead. I am happy. I haven't stopped enjoying life."

"You've said that already," Shirish replied quietly.

"But I didn't tell you one thing..." She paused, her eyes moist. "I loved you too. I still miss you. And perhaps... this feeling of missing you will ache my heart for the rest of my life."

The words hit Shirish like a wave. He had waited his whole life to hear them. He reached out and held her hands. She didn't resist. For a while, they just sat there, holding on to a fragile moment they knew would never return.

After fifteen minutes, they stood up to resume their journey towards the temple.

They walked in silence. So much was left unsaid between them, yet neither could find the words.

The temple was just one and a half kilometres away when Mini suddenly felt suffocated, clutching her chest lightly. The oxygen level was lower at this altitude. They sat on a big rock to rest.

"Please send my photos to me on Facebook Messenger," she requested.

"Don't you have WhatsApp?" he asked, pulling out his phone.

Mini smiled and showed him her old Nokia phone, a basic model, incapable of supporting WhatsApp.

He opened Facebook on his smartphone. She typed her name in the search bar, and her profile appeared instantly. He sent her a friend request and shared all the photos, including the one where they stood together, side by side.

She immediately requested him, "Please delete that one."

He deleted it, and then asked curiously, "Why?"

She smiled and said, "My husband is very possessive. If he saw that photo, he would divorce me."

Shirish frowned slightly. "He doesn't trust you?" he taunted.

Mini understood the hurt behind his words. She answered calmly, "Maybe you didn't listen carefully. He's a state-level wrestler. If someone even looks at me wrongly, he will break their bones, and he actually has."

"You're trying to scare me," Shirish said, laughing half-heartedly. "But remember... true lovers aren't afraid of anyone."

He had started with a laugh but ended with tears welling up in his eyes. Mini's eyes glistened too.

She whispered, "Please move forward in life. Time doesn't return. And... I can't come back to you."

Shirish's voice trembled as he asked, "May I... hug you once?"

"Here?!" she exclaimed, glancing around. He realised immediately: it wasn't possible.

"This... will remain my debt to you. I promise I'll repay it someday," she said softly.

Finally, they reached the temple.

Mini's mother-in-law and family were waiting. Shirish bowed and touched her feet respectfully, and shook hands with Mini's husband, a tall, muscular man, just as she had described. Mini's daughters were adorable, full of innocent energy.

"Who is he?" her mother-in-law asked curiously.

"He used to live in front of Mini's house. He's like her elder brother," Mini's husband replied casually.

Mini couldn't suppress her smile when she heard the introduction, 'elder brother'. That smile, full of mischief and emotion, was more precious to Shirish than anything he could ever possess.

She moved towards the temple with her family.

Shirish stood there, frozen like a statue. Once again, she had taken everything from him and yet, left him with everything too.

Tears betrayed his efforts to remain strong, sliding silently down his cheeks.

"Brother, why are you standing there? We're waiting in the queue," came his brother's voice.

"Nothing... I was just looking at you," Shirish replied, forcing a smile, and he walked towards the temple, carrying a lifetime of memories with every step.

XIV

June 2023

Mr Ratan Singh, the SHO of the city police station, was working on the theory of personal enmity, while Devraj focused on the serial killer angle. This division of work had been suggested by CO Singh, a seasoned officer known for her sharp instincts. She had made this arrangement to save time and reach a conclusion as quickly as possible.

Devraj headed to Nitin's office for the investigation. Nitin, a prominent businessman, owned a four-storey building. Two floors had been converted into a depot, while one was reserved for administrative staff. His personal office was located on the same administrative floor. The entire premises were under 24/7 CCTV surveillance.

Nitin was a dedicated businessman, spending almost ten hours a day in his establishment. During those hours, he interacted with numerous agents, customers, and suppliers. It made detecting a potential suspect through CCTV footage a tedious task.

Devraj spent hours reviewing footage from all available camera angles but found no suspicious person or activity. Still, he downloaded the footage from the last two days for deeper analysis.

Saturday came. The CO summoned Devraj and SHO Ratan Singh for a review meeting. She was eager to hear their progress.

Ratan Singh reported first, standing upright with the confidence of an officer who had left no stone unturned.

"Madam, in the past week, we investigated all possible angles of personal enmity. Nitin had no known disputes. He was his father's only son, and his two sisters are married into reputed business families. There is no property dispute, no visible rivalry. Family relationships are cordial."

The CO nodded appreciatively. "Great work, Ratan Singh ji."

She then turned to Devraj. "And what about your investigation, Devraj ji?"

"Madam, I thoroughly reviewed the CCTV footage of the last two days at Nitin's office, but found no suspicious activity or person," Devraj said, projecting the footage on to the screen for her.

CO Kavita Singh watched the clips attentively, sometimes pausing, rewinding, or making notes. After a few minutes, she leaned back and said, "You are correct, Devraj ji. There's nothing unusual here."

She closed the file, and then asked, "Is there anything else you discovered this week?"

"Yes, madam," Devraj said, his voice gaining an edge of excitement. "I investigated the relationship between Nitin and Vijay." He pulled out a set of call records. "I attempted to retrieve their call details.

Fortunately, Inspector Farrukh Ali, the previous investigating officer for Vijay's missing case, had already obtained Vijay's call history. Interestingly, Nitin's number appeared multiple times in Vijay's call records, although the duration of each call was usually only two to three minutes."

He placed the records before her.

She reviewed them carefully, her brows furrowing slightly. "So, you've concluded there was a connection between Nitin and Vijay? We already know they were acquainted."

Devraj leaned forward slightly. "Madam, please notice the pattern. This type of communication, frequent, short calls, is typical of operational exchanges: informing, updating, ordering, or delivering. But Vijay wasn't running any legitimate business. He was one of the prime accused in a blackmailing racket."

He let the silence sink in for a moment.

The CO's eyes gleamed. "Interesting. Are you suggesting that Nitin, directly or indirectly, could also have been involved in the blackmailing case?"

"Exactly, madam," Devraj said. "And if that is the motive behind the murder..." he hesitated for a second, "...then I'm afraid we should expect more murders in the near future."

For a moment, the room went still.

Kavita sat back in her chair, impressed by the depth of his analysis.

"Devraj ji," she said finally, "your next step is to collect the details of every victim involved in the blackmailing case. Also, dig deeper into the profiles of all the accused, not just the ones convicted. There must be others hiding in the shadows."

"Yes, madam," Devraj saluted smartly, ready to leave.

Before he could step out, she added, her tone serious, "Devraj ji, we must speed up. The murderer must have realised by now that he can no longer hide his tracks by choosing victims across different police station jurisdictions."

Then, turning to both officers, she said, "Ratan Singh ji, Devraj ji, share all your findings with each other. From now on, you must work as one team. This case is about more than just justice; it's about the reputation of the police department itself."

"Yes, madam!" both officers said in unison, saluting smartly before exiting the room with a renewed sense of urgency.

***

Devraj was stationed at the same police station where Inspector Farrukh Ali had once worked. Farrukh had conducted the initial investigation into the blackmailing case and had compiled a list of seven accused. Out of these seven, four were in jail, two had been murdered, and the seventh was unnamed.

This missing culprit had been listed by Farrukh Ali as the 'main accused' in his records, but strangely, he had never mentioned the name anywhere. When Devraj discovered this gap, he immediately informed the CO.

The CO took the matter seriously. "Meet Farrukh Ali," she instructed firmly. "Find out everything you can."

Devraj dug into Farrukh Ali's history. It took some effort, but eventually, he uncovered grim news: Farrukh Ali had passed away the previous summer, reportedly from a heart attack. The information was confirmed when Devraj visited his home and spoke briefly with the family.

Later, Devraj sat across from the CO once again, seeking her guidance and confirmation that he was following the right trail.

"My instinct says that this unknown seventh man is the next target," Devraj told her. CO Kavita Singh had already arrived at the same conclusion.

"Devraj Ji," she said, "meet the families of those five girls who died by suicide after the blackmailing scandal. I have a suspicion, maybe the killer is connected to one of those families."

Without delay, Devraj set out. He met the families, though the task was far from easy. One family had moved to another city to escape the stigma. At first, they refused to meet him, fearing old wounds would be reopened. It took repeated visits and sincere efforts to earn their trust.

He learnt their tragic story: they had two daughters, and the elder one—the victim—had endured unspeakable humiliation after the blackmailing scandal surfaced. Their life was made miserable by local thugs. Devraj realised that this family, broken and reclusive, could not have been involved in any killings.

Devraj reached a similar conclusion after meeting all five families. Each visit revealed a heartbreaking pattern: families paralysed by fear of public disgrace, unable or unwilling to fight for justice for their daughters. The girls were not just victims of the blackmailers, but also of a society that imposed suffocating restrictions on their honour and freedom.

Expanding his investigation, Devraj revisited the families of all the people named in Farrukh Ali's old reports. It took him another week, but again, no leads. Most families were satisfied with the old police investigation and were reluctant to revisit the dark past.

After two exhausting weeks, Devraj found himself back in square one. Frustrated, he sat in his office, trying to piece the puzzle together once more. Then, an idea struck him, simple yet powerful.

He immediately called the CO. "Madam, I request permission to meet the accused currently in jail," he said.

Recognising the importance of the lead, Kavita approved his request without hesitation.

The next day, Devraj arrived at the district jail. The jail superintendent had already assured full cooperation. A room was arranged where Devraj could interrogate the accused one by one, without interference.

First came Ravi, then Akbar. They had once been branded as 'fast friends', but Devraj quickly sensed the truth: there were cracks among them. During the questioning, Ravi exploded with anger, accusing Vijay of being the real culprit behind the blackmailing ring. Devraj, carefully playing on their bitterness, dropped another name casually, "And what about Nitin?"

Akbar immediately picked up the thread. "Nitin sponsored many of Vijay and Rahul's dirty games," he said, bitterness dripping from his voice.

Gradually, Devraj steered the conversation towards the mysterious seventh man. "And that man, what's his name... Ra... Rat...?" Devraj deliberately fumbled.

Akbar, caught off guard, blurted out, "Ajay! He's the nephew of Minister Vijay Pratap Singh."

Ravi nodded in agreement.

Bingo. Devraj had found the missing link. He concealed his excitement and played it cool. "Don't worry," he said casually. "Soon, even he will be behind bars."

As he stood to leave, Ravi and Akbar spoke up, their voices filled with sudden desperation, "Sir, we are innocent!"

Devraj stared at them coldly. "Go tell that to the parents of the girls whose lives you ruined."

Without wasting a minute, Devraj rushed back to the CO. He reported everything: the missing seventh man's identity, his political connections, and the complicated danger ahead. Ajay wasn't just anyone, he was the nephew of the former home minister Vijay Pratap Singh, who, though no longer holding that powerful portfolio, was still a heavyweight in the current cabinet.

Arresting Ajay openly could spark a political storm, especially since the blackmail case was still under trial in the high court. They knew Ajay was involved, but lacked evidence to convict him. For now, their priority was to save his life, because if the killer's motive was to eliminate the accused in the case, then he would surely be next. They tried calling him, but his phone was switched off. Panic set in, yet they avoided informing Ajay's family, as revealing the threat would not only alarm them but might also tip off the murderer.

CO Kavita Singh and Devraj decided on a delicate approach: they would meet Minister Vijay Pratap Singh personally. After consulting their seniors, they secured an appointment within hours.

It immediately deepened the concern of the CO and Devraj. Without wasting time, Devraj asked the minister if he knew where Ajay had gone. Vijay Pratap, still on call with his brother, relayed the question, but the answer was disappointing.

"He often goes on outings like this, without informing anyone," the brother said vaguely. They requested Ajay's mobile number. Devraj dialled it on the spot; the line was out of reach.

The CO made a quick decision. "We'll have to put his number on surveillance," she informed the minister bluntly. Though visibly uncomfortable, Vijay Pratap Singh did not object. He knew the gravity of the situation.

Kavita immediately called her surveillance team and ordered Ajay's number to be traced and tracked. Before leaving, she reminded the minister, "Please, inform us immediately if you hear anything from him, any message, any location."

As soon as they stepped outside, she instructed the driver to head straight to the police headquarters.

During the ride, she issued fresh orders: all nearby police stations bordering the city must intensify patrolling, set up random vehicle checks, and discreetly keep an eye on all movements, especially near forested and less populated areas.

"Madam," Devraj asked, his voice heavy with doubt, "do you still think he will choose this area again?"

The CO looked out of the car window, her face tense. "Devraj ji, we can only hope. We don't have a lead about his movements. We have to prepare for all possibilities."

The next few days blurred into a relentless hunt. Day and night, their teams worked, checking highways, scanning CCTV footage from toll booths, questioning informants, checking mobile networks for any stray signals.

Then, one grim morning, they received news, but it wasn't the news they had hoped for. Ajay's body had been found, dumped in a jungle near the very area they had been guarding so fiercely.

XV

June 2013

After returning from Kedarnath, Shirish got busy with his routine life. Yet, he carried back many beautiful memories—memories of breathtaking sceneries, warm moments shared with family, and most vividly, the time spent with her. The memories lived in his mobile phone in the form of photos. Most were casual captures he barely glanced at. But there were a few he visited often, the ones of Mini.

Though he had moved on after her marriage years ago, convincing himself that time had healed everything, the Kedarnath trip had turned everything upside down. Her face lingered in his mind's eye, stubborn and vivid. She began appearing in his dreams again, almost every night now. It had happened before, but not with such persistence.

It was June 2013. The news of devastating floods in Kedarnath flashed across every TV screen. Shirish, like everyone else, watched in stunned silence. The places he had once walked through, the roads, the temples, the bustling lanes, were now scenes of ruin. Family members called him, checking on each other. A sense of helplessness and sadness enveloped him.

That night, scrolling mindlessly through Facebook, drowning deeper in melancholy, he was about to log out when a notification popped up on Messenger.

A single word: *Hi!*

From Mini.

His heart skipped a beat. He replied immediately, though a glance at the timestamp showed she had sent it hours ago, at 4 p.m. He felt a pang of regret for seeing it so late.

He waited hopefully, but there was no immediate reply. Disappointed, he was about to close the app when the screen displayed: Seen. Moments later, a message came: *How are you?*

He responded quickly: *Fine! And you?*

Me too. I'll talk to you in the morning, she replied.

Eager not to end the conversation, he sent a few more casual hellos, but they remained unread. Anxious, he spent a restless night. By morning, he had checked Messenger at least twenty times, each time facing disappointment.

Around 4 p.m. the next day, while trapped in a meeting, his phone buzzed with the messenger notification tone he had especially set for her. Torn between duty and desire, he excused himself, citing the washroom, and rushed out.

Inside, he found her message. She apologised for not responding the previous night, explaining that she had been with her husband, who didn't like her using her phone when he was around. They slipped into a conversation about the Kedarnath floods, memories weaving through the unfolding tragedy and the happier times they had shared there. Shirish lost track of time. Only the shrill ring of his phone—*his boss was calling*—snapped him back. Flustered, he apologised to Mini, promising to return, and hurried back to the meeting, covering his absence by blaming a "disturbed stomach".

That evening, he checked Messenger again. She wasn't online, but she had left a message:

Will talk tomorrow.

The next day, a strange mix of anxiety and excitement gnawed at him. He kept glancing at the clock. By 4 p.m., he could no longer hold back and opened Messenger. She appeared around 4.15 p.m. and sent a cheerful: *Hi!*

He quickly replied: *You're late!*

Late? Really? I have household chores and responsibilities to handle, she answered lightly.

I waited for fifteen minutes, he grumbled.

Please understand, Shirish. I can join only when I'm free. My life isn't mine alone any more.

Feeling slighted, he impulsively wrote: *Please be on time from now onwards.*

Her reply came, sharp and cutting: *See, I'm not your girlfriend. I'm a wife and a mother of two daughters. I love my family.*

Then, she disappeared.

Though just a chat, her words stung. Shirish stared at the screen, anger and embarrassment rising. His fingers hovered over a harsh reply; he even typed it out, but then paused. *No.* Harshness would only hurt him more.

Taking a deep breath, he instead typed: *Sorry.*

There was no response. Minutes crawled by. He sent another soft, *Sorry.*

Feeling hollow and defeated, he sat staring blankly at the screen.

Suddenly, the messenger ringtone chimed. It was her.

My daughter had taken the phone to call her friend. I just saw your message. You don't need to say sorry.

Relief flooded him.

He quickly wrote, *I thought I'd lost the chance to talk to you.*

Mini replied thoughtfully: *Shirish, I'm afraid I'm giving you false hope. I'm talking to you only as a friend. Please remember that.*

The words pierced him, but he clung to whatever thread he had.

I'm not interested in anyone's wife, he joked and sent a teasing emoji.

She replied with laughing emojis. Then she sent him a few images: haunting pictures of the flooded Kedarnath.

They chatted about the disaster, slipping into lighter memories of their own trip. For an hour, they shared photos, stories, laughter—a moment suspended between the past and the present.

Before leaving, she asked sweetly, *May I talk to you again tomorrow?*

Shirish's heart swelled. *I'll be waiting*, he replied.

It was the beginning of something that Shirish had once only dared to dream about. Back when Mini was unmarried, he had never found the courage to speak much to her. Now, after all these years, through chats and stolen moments online, he was living the conversations he had once craved.

Mini, however, made it clear time and again that this was just friendship. Shirish heard her words, but his heart chose to ignore the reminders.

Gradually, their chatting time stretched longer. Both became habituated with each other. Whenever they could steal a moment from their busy lives, they exchanged messages, little fragments of their day reserved for one another.

Mini often urged him to get married. Sometimes she sent pictures of girls, hoping he'd choose one. They discussed each girl endlessly, but Shirish always found a reason to reject her.

One day, laughing, Mini warned him, *Don't compare every girl to me.*

He teased back, *Don't flatter yourself so much!*

Sometimes she grew upset, sometimes he turned rude. It was a delicate line somewhere between innocent friendship and silent, forbidden longing.

***

In 2015, one afternoon, Shirish sent her a message: *Get ready for a video call!*

Messenger had just launched its video-calling feature. Mini refused instantly, but Shirish, mischievous and insistent, kept trying. She rejected the calls, again and again. Angry and hurt, Shirish went silent for two days. By the third day, he realised he couldn't stay away from her for long.

She has a family. She won't even miss me, he thought bitterly, but it only hurt more. When he finally opened Messenger, he found a message waiting for him: *Sorry, Uncle! How long will you stay angry with me?*

The word 'uncle' teased him, but the affection hidden behind it melted him completely. Tears welled up in his eyes. It was the first time he truly felt he meant something to her. He read the message again and again, trying to imagine her voice, her smile.

He replied playfully: *Aunty, can I call you now?*

Uncle, you're crazy! Call me at 4 p.m., she laughed back.

At 4 p.m. sharp, Shirish made the call. After so long, he saw her, blurred through a poor network, but beautiful as ever. That small, imperfect call kept him thrilled for days. Video calls became more frequent after that. Sometimes she answered, sometimes she left the call unanswered, and he understood, but not always willingly.

One evening, during a video chat, Shirish reminded her of an old promise she had once made.

Mini looked puzzled. He gently prompted her, reminding her of the time, the place, but she pretended not to recall. He pushed twice or thrice, but when she continued pretending, he dropped the topic, wounded inside. He could not dare to say the words aloud. Mini understood, but she didn't want to encourage it either.

As time passed, Shirish's desire to meet her grew stronger. Meanwhile, Mini felt trapped. This emotional tie was growing too strong, and it was starting to choke her married life. Fear gnawed at her. She knew she had to end it before it was too late.

One day, summoning all her courage, she sent him a message: *Need to talk. Please call.*

She sent her phone number and the time to call. Shirish's heart raced; he thought it was a step closer, a deeper trust between them. When he called, he thanked her profusely for trusting him with her number. Mini regretted it almost immediately. She realised it would not be easy to convince him to end this. Shirish spoke a lot. She listened silently, patiently. Finally, he murmured, "Say something... My ears are eager to hear your sweet voice."

Her voice, when it came, was heavy. "Shirish, you might not like what I have to say."

"What?" he asked, oblivious.

"I'm feeling uneasy," she whispered.

"Are you okay? Are you sick?" he asked, panicking.

"I'm fine," she reassured him. "It's because of... this relationship."

Silence stretched between them.

"Which relationship?" he asked, though deep down he knew.

"Ours," she said firmly. "I want to end it."

Each word was a hammer striking his heart. He had always feared this end, but hearing it shattered him. He tried desperately to convince her, to plead with her, but Mini was determined. The call ended bitterly, full of heavy words and broken silences. For fifteen days, they did not speak.

Mini thought Shirish had finally accepted the reality. She missed him at times, but trained herself to move on. Then, one day, a weeping emoji popped up from him on Messenger. She deleted it without replying. She tried focusing on other things but found herself unable to resist. Finally, unable to bear it, she messaged: *What happened?*

Instead of replying in words, Shirish called. This time, she answered. He was crying. Helplessly, she consoled him. The dam broke. Their old routine resumed. She knew it was dangerous, but her heart couldn't resist the pull.

One day, he brought up her old promise again. This time, he was stubborn. He said directly: *You had promised me a hug.*

Mini tried to deny it. Shirish insisted, pleaded, demanded. She tried to resist, but he was relentless. Finally, she agreed, but only on one condition. *This will be the last time we meet*, she said, trembling.

Mini's heart was torn. Her mind told her to run away, but her emotions, tangled and heavy, held her back. They decided on a time and place. When she arrived, she realised Shirish had booked a hotel room.

She frowned, uneasy. “Why here? We could have met at a park,” she said.

“A park isn’t safe,” he explained softly. “Imagine if someone saw us. You could regret it later. I don’t want you to regret this meeting, ever.”

“And what if someone sees me here, walking into a hotel?” she asked, her voice low.

But strangely, even as her mind screamed at her to leave, her feet stayed. She followed him to the room. They stayed for more than two hours, talking, laughing, crying, hugging, and stealing what little time they could from the world. When she finally left, she carried a strange, aching mix of happiness and guilt. That evening, Shirish received a message from her, a simple heart emoji. It said everything her words could not.

XVI

July 2023

Devraj sat at his desk, staring at Ajay's postmortem report. He didn't want to open it.

He already knew what it would say.

The pressure was suffocating from his seniors, the public, and especially the politicians. Ajay belonged to a powerful political family. His death had turned into the most sensational news story across newspapers and TV channels.

Just then, his phone buzzed. It was a call from the CO. Devraj knew exactly why she was calling. Sighing, he picked up the report, mounted his bike, and sped towards her office. Ratan Singh was waiting outside when he arrived. They exchanged a brief smile, a smile that needed no words. It spoke of the storm they were both caught in.

Inside, CO Kavita Singh gestured for them to sit. For a moment, silence hung heavy in the room.

Then she said, her voice calm but steely, "Devraj ji, Ratan Singh ji, we have very little time. The CBI can take over this case any day now. We can look at this situation in two ways, either as a way to get rid of a headache, or as a black spot on our pride. I, for one, take it as a black spot. You may decide for yourselves."

Ratan Singh didn't hesitate. "Madam, we are with you. We won't leave a single stone unturned," he said firmly. Devraj nodded, echoing his commitment.

Singh continued, "Then, we must proceed with complete focus. There's something we're missing, something not yet visible. Look at it: five murders. One motive. If we find that motive, we can crack this case. These murders are connected, but how?"

Devraj, deep in thought, spoke carefully, "Madam, if we consider the motive linked to a faulty investigation, which is quite evident, then at least we can explain the murder of Inspector Devendra Kumar."

"Yes, madam, Devraj is right," Ratan Singh added. "But how do we tie Dr Prakash into this?"

A slight smile played on the CO's face. She leaned forward and asked, "What was Dr Prakash's job profile?"

"He was a professor of anatomy in a medical college," Devraj replied.

"Anything else?" she pressed.

"He also conducted postmortems when required," Devraj added.

"Exactly," she said, tapping her fingers lightly on the table.

Ratan Singh let out a deep sigh as realisation dawned on him.

"You both are brilliant," she said warmly. "The key is hidden in a faulty investigation, probably a murder case. Look at the pattern: the killings have similarities, blood loss, precise cuts to the veins... techniques an anatomy professor would know too well." She continued, her voice rising with conviction, "The time span of these murders is around three to three and a half years. After each crime, the killer waited until things calmed down before striking again. Except for the last two, where he moved faster. It suggests two possibilities: either he's trying to finish his list before we catch him, or he's done and is now planning his escape."

The room fell silent, each of them lost in thought. Finally, Devraj spoke, "So, we need to gather the records of all murders across the entire area. Madam, for that, we'll need your intervention; please instruct all the police stations that share boundaries with our area. It'll save us a lot of time. I'll collect the records from my station."

"And I'll collect the records from mine," Ratan Singh chimed in.

"Good. We meet back here at 8.30 p.m.," Kavita said.

Ratan Singh looked surprised. "Madam, 8.30 p.m.?"

"Yes, Ratan Singh ji," she said firmly. "We don't have the luxury of wasting even a single hour."

***

In the evening, they gathered again at the CO's office. On her table was a towering pile of case files. She looked puzzled, even a little overwhelmed, seeing the sheer number of them. Devraj couldn't help but smile at her expression.

Noticing his smile, she frowned. "Devraj ji, since you find this so amusing, it's your duty to study all these files and select the relevant ones," she said sharply.

Devraj chuckled and replied, "Madam, I already have a file that I believe you must see before we dive into all this." He handed the file to her.

She took it and asked, "Which case is this? And why do you think it's connected?"

"Madam," Devraj said, "you might remember, about seven years ago, there was a case that shook the entire nation. This is that case."

"Devraj ji," she said, "there have been quite a few cases that have shaken either the state or the nation since I joined."

At this, both Devraj and Ratan Singh laughed, and she joined them, lightening the mood briefly.

"Which case, exactly?" she asked again, smiling now.

"The famous 'Sabala' case," Devraj answered.

"The Sabala case! But that's still under trial. The accused is in jail. If I'm not wrong, the sessions court has already given its verdict, and now the appeal is in the high court," she said, surprised.

"Yes, madam, exactly," Devraj confirmed.

"Then why are you so eager to revisit it?" she asked, her tone sceptical.

"Madam, there's a general opinion, even among officers, that the investigation in that case was rushed, maybe even mishandled," Devraj explained.

The CO's face tightened. "Devraj ji, are we setting investigation lines based on public opinion now?" she said, irritated.

"Madam," Devraj said respectfully, "I'm not deviating from the direction we agreed upon this morning. I truly believe this case has the highest possibility of a faulty investigation, and it aligns with our leads."

"Why do you think so?" she probed, unconvinced.

"First," Devraj said calmly, "the cause of death: heavy blood loss. Second, the location. Sabala's body was found in the same general area where the other victims' bodies were discovered. Third, the investigating officer, guess who it was?"

"Devendra Kumar?" she guessed, her eyes widening.

Devraj nodded. "And the doctor who conducted the postmortem?"

"Dr Prakash!" she almost shouted.

"Yes, madam." Devraj nodded, smiling slightly.

The CO sat back, stunned. "My goodness! How did you find this case like a needle in a haystack?!"

"Madam, there's a constable in my station, Ram Pratap. He's the most senior there, posted for the last five years. To save time, I discussed our case pattern with him. He casually mentioned a few cases, and while talking, this one slipped out. His body language afterwards gave it away. He tried to backtrack and hide details. That made me suspicious," Devraj explained.

"Good work, Devraj ji," she said, genuinely impressed.

They sat together and began studying the Sabala case file. It didn't take long to spot multiple loopholes:

- According to the case diary, the accused, Chatar Singh had brought Sabala to the crime scene in a van, yet there were no photographs of tyre marks at the scene.
- If he had to enter the school premises, the gate must have been locked. So how did he open it without stopping the van?
- Why didn't the victim attempt to escape from the vehicle?
- Was someone already at the spot, or inside the van, helping Chatar Singh control her?

Questions stacked up rapidly.

"I think you're right, Devraj ji," CO Kavita Singh said seriously. "This case could be the key connection to the current murders." She turned to Ratan Singh. "Ratan Singh ji, your job is to meet all the original witnesses from the Sabala case. Try to find anything, any cracks in their statements. Devraj ji, you go to the district jail and meet Chatar Singh. Try to get something useful from him."

They nodded and dispersed quickly.

The next day, the real work began. Ratan Singh met all the listed witnesses. With his experience, it didn't take him long to understand: the witnesses had been created, coached and planted. He even recognised one of them: a man with a record of providing false testimonies for money. He reported all these findings to the CO immediately.

Meanwhile, Devraj reached the district jail to meet Chatar Singh. He had to arrange a special permit for the meeting. At first, Chatar Singh refused to speak. He sat silently, a stubborn glint in his eyes.

Devraj, thinking quickly, decided to bait him. “It’s your choice, Chatar Singh,” he said casually, “whether you talk or not. But just know this: the department has already found serious loopholes in the original investigation. A fresh inquiry will start soon. If you really were falsely accused, this might be your last chance to set the record straight...”

Chatar Singh looked up sharply.

Devraj leaned forward slightly, his voice steady but sharp. “Reinvestigation is happening, Chatar Singh. This time, the focus is different. There’s a chance to uncover the truth. If you’re innocent, this could help you too.”

Chatar Singh’s eyes filled with tears. “Innocent?” he said bitterly, his voice cracking. “My only fault was that I had dropped her at the school. Nothing else.” He broke down, weeping bitterly.

Devraj stared at him, stunned. “What are you saying?” he asked carefully.

“Yes... it’s true...” Chatar Singh sobbed. “But the police had already decided to trap me. They created false witnesses against me. No one was ready to listen to my side.”

Devraj gave him a few seconds to collect himself, and then asked gently, “Tell me clearly, did Sabala hire you to take her to the school, or was it someone else?”

Chatar Singh wiped his tears with the back of his hand and replied, "That afternoon, a man came to me. He offered me a job, to transport a woman from a point to the school. At first, I refused; it was a distant place, far from my usual route. But when he offered me Rs 1,000 for the ride, greed got the better of me. It was a big amount for me then." He paused, recalling the day in fragments.

Devraj nodded, absorbing every word. "Didn't you find it suspicious, a woman alone, late at night?" he asked.

"At that time," Chatar Singh said, lowering his eyes, "I just thought she might be a prostitute. The man's casual attitude, the money, everything pointed that way. I didn't ask questions. I just did what I was paid to do."

Devraj tapped his pen lightly on his notebook, and then asked, "What did you do when you heard about her murder?"

"I found out through a video on WhatsApp. As soon as I saw it, I panicked. I realised the police might connect me to it. I got scared and ran away to my native village. That was my biggest mistake. Running away made me look guilty," Chatar Singh said, shame washing over his face.

Devraj leaned in a bit more. "Do you know the man who gave you the Rs 1000?" he asked.

Chatar Singh shook his head sadly. "Back then, I dealt with so many faces every day that I never thought of memorising any of them. And the police twisted this, said I was lying, that I was making up a story. They used it to break me in court."

Devraj sat silently for a moment, piecing the puzzle together. Finally, he asked the big question,

"In your opinion, why did the police trap you?"

Chatar Singh let out a hollow, bitter laugh. "What can I say? Maybe they needed a scapegoat. Maybe they needed to close the case quickly. And I was easy to frame, a poor van driver, without connections, without power."

A deep silence settled between them. Devraj stood up, understanding now that the rabbit hole was far deeper than he had imagined.

"Thank you, Chatar Singh. Maybe this time, justice will find its way," he said and left.

***

In the evening, CO Kavita Singh, Devraj, and Ratan Singh gathered at her office once again. They had spent the day gathering crucial pieces of information, but a lingering sense of urgency remained. The weight of the investigation grew heavier with each passing moment as the realisation of how deep the rot ran became more apparent.

The CO sat at her desk, flipping through the reports, her mind focused. She raised her head to look at the two officers standing before her. Ratan Singh and Devraj exchanged glances, aware that the time had come for the next phase of the investigation.

After a long pause, she spoke, her voice low but filled with resolve, "So, it's clear now. Inspector Devendra Kumar did not conduct the investigation honestly. Instead, he used all his energy to suppress the matter. He presented a fake accused to the public, and ironically, the court sentenced the wrong man to capital punishment."

Ratan Singh nodded solemnly, "Yes, madam. He used every means at his disposal to frame an innocent man."

Her fingers tapped on the file in front of her as she continued, "But why did he do this? What motivated his actions?"

Ratan Singh spoke up, "Could it have been money? Perhaps he was paid to do this."

Kavita frowned. "I don't think so. Devendra Kumar wasn't a fool. He wouldn't have taken such a big risk for money alone. There has to be another reason."

Devraj, deep in thought, added, "Maybe it was political pressure. That seems to make sense."

The CO's eyes sharpened as the pieces began to fall into place. "Yes, you're right. Political pressure. But the question remains: who could have wielded that much influence?"

Without hesitation, Devraj answered, "Ex-home minister, Shri Vijay Pratap Singh. He's the one who could have influenced the investigation."

Kavita's face tightened as the weight of the realisation hit her. "Yes, it's obvious now. Ajay was involved in this case with Nitin and Vijay. Vijay Pratap Singh took advantage of his position to influence the investigation and cover up the real culprits. As a result, the murderer was able to escape justice."

The room fell silent for a moment as the gravity of the situation settled over them. Ratan Singh hesitated, then spoke, his voice filled with concern, "Madam, we know the murderer killed Dr Prakash for manipulating the report, and Devendra Kumar for his role in letting the real culprit go free. The question now is: will he go after Vijay Pratap Singh next?"

Devraj finished the thought, "It's highly likely. The murderer has been cleaning up all the loose ends. He won't stop until he gets to the top."

The CO stood up sharply, her eyes narrowing in determination. "We can't take any chances. We need to take immediate action. We must protect Shri Vijay Pratap Singh at all costs."

Ratan Singh, ever the realist, muttered, "But he won't cooperate. He's too proud, and he refuses to admit to his misdeeds."

The CO looked at him with firm resolve. "He will cooperate. We'll makc sure of that. We'll restart the investigation, but first, we need to protect him."

The next day, she went to meet the superintendent and briefed him on the situation and the confirmed threat to Vijay Pratap Singh's life. "Sir, we've received credible information that Shri Vijay Pratap Singh is in danger. We need to arrange immediate protection for him."

The superintendent nodded grimly. "Kavita ji, do whatever you need to. Make sure his safety is guaranteed."

She responded with a slight nod. "Thank you, sir. But I need one favour. He already has security, but if we tell him the full extent of the threat, it might cause unnecessary panic. Could you inform him discreetly and ask him to cooperate with us?"

The superintendent agreed. "I'll take care of it. Leave it to me."

That evening, the three officers went to meet with Vijay Pratap Singh at his residence. When they arrived, he was seated comfortably, his posture as arrogant as ever. The moment they entered, he flashed a mocking, sarcastic smile. "Ah, the infamous trio. The same officers who couldn't save my nephew Ajay. How do I know you'll be able to save me? Maybe I should make my own arrangements."

"Yes, sir, we've heard many stories about your time in power, how you dealt with the police," Ratan Singh said in a way that seemed like a compliment, though the other two officers knew what he truly meant.

"This is all dirty politics. You will never receive any appreciation for your good work. Now, tell me the plan and the level of threat," Vijay Pratap Singh said, his voice laced with disdain.

"Sir, we know that you already have security. We just want to add some of our people to your team. We've received information that the person who killed Mr Ajay may target you in the coming days. We cannot take this lightly. So, until we catch him, we need your cooperation," CO Kavita Singh explained.

"All right, so whom do you want to deploy in my security?" he asked, still sounding sceptical but willing to cooperate.

"Mr Ratan Singh will be the person overseeing your security. Ratan Singh ji, I want regular updates from you," she ordered.

"Yes, madam!" Ratan Singh replied, his tone respectful.

The CO left Devraj at his police station and returned to her office. She instructed the orderly to bring her a cup of tea, hoping to relax before heading home. Just as she was about to leave, the phone in her office rang. She picked it up reluctantly.

"You've done a lot of work today," a voice on the other side whispered.

"Who are you?" she asked, instantly alert.

"Madam, I'm the same person you've been searching for."

CO Kavita Singh gestured for the orderly to send someone to her office.

"Madam, don't try to trace me. You won't reach me in fifteen minutes. I'm calling from a PCO. You can't catch me. So, if you want to talk, I'll continue; but if you want to try and catch me, I'll hang up immediately," the caller warned.

"Speak," she said calmly. Her subordinate entered the office, and she quickly wrote on a piece of paper: "Trace the call." He hurried out to carry out her orders.

"You can't save him. Do whatever you want," the caller taunted.

"I suggest you surrender. We're reopening the Sabala case. I promise you, we will send each and every culprit behind bars," she said firmly.

"I know how you people do investigations," came the reply with a cold laugh. "I assure you, I won't leave a single culprit alive for you. You won't have to do any hard work."

"Believe me, I'm not like the officers you've dealt with before," she responded, hoping to keep him talking long enough for her men to trace his location.

"I know that," he said. "That's why I'm talking to you. If I fail, it will be a regret for me, but you'll regret your life. He's not a man who deserves any respect."

"The law doesn't allow me to judge anyone based on their deeds. If he's the culprit, I must present him in court, especially alive. And I will do that," she challenged.

Her subordinate signalled that they needed five more minutes of conversation.

"I know your capacity, but believe me, this time, you will fail," he said, his voice oozing with arrogance. Then, without further warning, he hung up.

"Hello?" she said into the phone, but there was no response.

She immediately called Devraj and instructed him to come to her office as soon as possible. Devraj, who was on his way home, turned his bike around and arrived at the CO's office in fifteen minutes. All the officers were gathered there. She instructed him to sit and handed him a file to review.

"What's going on, madam?" he asked.

"I got a call from the killer."

"What? Really?" Devraj asked, his eyes widening in surprise. "Can we trace his location?"

"No, we can't," one of the officers answered.

"I knew we wouldn't be able to trace him," Devraj said knowingly.

"How do you know that?" the CO asked, intrigued.

"His track record tells us this. He plans everything perfectly. He won't allow us to trace him. He has some reason for calling you," he replied.

"Devraj, we have to stop him. If I'm not wrong, he has ways of keeping an eye on us," she said, her anxiety creeping into her words.

"Madam, we need to check everyone who's close to Vijay Pratap Singh. You deployed security today, and immediately after that, you got the call," Devraj suggested.

The CO immediately called Ratan Singh and instructed him to send over a list of everyone close to Vijay Pratap Singh. She also ordered him to arrange a meeting with all those people as soon as possible.

Turning to Devraj, she added, "The killer must be someone close to Sabala's family, maybe her husband or her brother. Devraj, meet with her family tomorrow as early as possible."

"Okay, madam!"

"You may leave now. Meet me at 11 a.m. Try to meet her family before you come here," she instructed him.

***

Devraj stood at the door of Sabala's house and rang the bell. A girl, around thirteen years old and wearing a school uniform, opened the gate. She looked up at him, confused.

"May I speak with your father?" he asked.

"Dad, someone wants to meet you," the girl said, looking scared at the sight of him in his police uniform.

A bodybuilder-like man appeared at the gate. "Yes?" he asked.

"Mr Narendra Kumar, I am Inspector Devraj. I need to talk to you for a few minutes," Devraj introduced himself.

"About what?" Narendra asked, his tone harsh.

"I want to talk to you about the murder of your wife."

"Now, after all these years? And what's the logic behind this now? I'm busy. I need to drop my daughter at school. I can't talk right now," Narendra said, his rudeness evident.

"Go ahead and drop your daughter off. I'll wait for you. This is important, and I'm sure you'd prefer not to come down to the station to answer some routine questions," Devraj said, matching Narendra's tone.

Devraj entered the house and sat on the sofa. Narendra, realising he couldn't get rid of Devraj without answering him, called his neighbour to arrange for someone to drop his daughter at school. After a few moments, he turned to Devraj. "Ask whatever you need to," he said reluctantly.

"Have you dropped your daughter off at school?" Devraj asked.

"I've arranged for someone to take her. Now, please, just ask your questions," Narendra responded impatiently.

Devraj showed him photos of Nitin, Ajay, and Vijay. "Do you know these people?" he asked.

"Who are they?" Narendra replied, though Devraj noticed a subtle change in his expression.

"Do you know Mr Vijay Pratap Singh?" Devraj pressed.

"The former home minister? Who in the city doesn't know him?" Narendra replied, his tone dismissive.

"How do you know him?"

"Like everyone else does," Narendra replied. "I heard he took a special interest in the case of my wife's murder," he added, his voice a little more guarded.

"Any other reason for knowing him?"

"Yes, I will never forget some of his favours," Narendra said, his tone softening a bit.

"What kind of favours?" Devraj pressed.

"If I start counting, I could tell you," Narendra said cryptically.

"Are you satisfied with the investigation into your wife's murder?" Devraj asked, shifting the topic.

"You've come here to ask me this?" Narendra responded irritably.

"I need an answer," Devraj replied, his own tone growing harsher with frustration.

"You and your investigations!" Narendra sneered. "I saw how your investigation went. The real culprit escaped, and your officers framed someone who was probably innocent."

"Do you know who the real culprit is? Do you have any suspicions about anyone?"

"If I knew who the culprit was, I'd make sure they were punished in a way that served as a lesson to other criminals," Narendra said, his fists clenched in anger.

"Where were you on these dates?" Devraj asked, handing him a list of dates.

"How am I supposed to remember? These are old dates," Narendra said dismissively.

"Try to remember. Maybe something will come back to you," Devraj insisted.

"I can't remember," Narendra said flatly.

"Try harder!" Devraj urged.

"I can't remember. Do you have any more questions? If not, I really need to get back to work," Narendra snapped, growing more irritated.

"I'm leaving now, but we'll meet again," Devraj said, turning to walk away. Then, he paused and turned. "Where is your wife's brother?"

"He's in America, working there. Why do you ask? Are you planning to go meet him in the US?" Narendra shot back sarcastically.

Devraj left the house and headed to the CO's office. She was waiting for him when he arrived.

"Have you met the family?" she asked.

"Yes, madam. He could be a potential suspect."

"How can you say that?" she asked, eager for details.

"Madam, he's a state-level wrestler, about six foot three inches tall. He has no faith in the police investigation. He's rude when speaking to a policeman, and he knows that Mr Vijay Pratap Singh interfered in the investigation of his wife's murder," Devraj explained, summarising his reasons for suspicion. "Here's his number. Can we track his location on these dates?" he continued, handing her the details.

"Rajesh ji, please do this for us," she instructed one of her staff who handled these matters for the department.

"Devraj ji, come with me. I'm going to meet Mr Vijay Pratap Singh's staff," she said as she led him to the meeting.

They couldn't find anyone suspicious among Mr Vijay Pratap Singh's staff. Meanwhile, she received details about Narendra Kumar's location. He had been in the area on the possible date of Ajay and Nitin's abduction. She shared this information with Devraj.

"Madam, we shouldn't waste time. We should arrest him immediately. This is enough proof to apprehend him," Devraj suggested.

"Devraj ji and Ratan Singh ji, you stay here and keep a close watch. Don't let anyone meet Mr Vijay Pratap Singh without proper screening," she instructed, and sent officers to capture Narendra Kumar.

She met with Vijay Pratap Singh's secretary to learn about his schedule for the next few days. The secretary mentioned that he had meetings with several leaders and was scheduled to inaugurate a jewellery showroom and an exhibition in the evening.

"Is it important to inaugurate these events?" she asked.

"Yes, it's important. If the police aren't capable of providing protection, let me know. I can give my life for my people," Vijay Pratap Singh said as he descended the stairs.

"Okay, sir, please allow me to come with you," she replied.

"If you want to come, I welcome you. But do you really think it'll help? After all, you're a woman. How can you handle a man? Don't you think a male officer would be better for the job?" he taunted.

"Don't worry, the male officer will protect you. They'll remain outside the vehicle, but I will instruct them on what action to take," she responded calmly.

Vijay Pratap Singh felt an urge to slap her for her response, but controlled himself. Already embroiled in numerous controversies, he didn't want to create any further issues that could damage his reputation, especially with a promising political future. Reluctantly, he agreed for her to accompany him.

As her phone rang, she excused herself and answered the call. Her officers, sent to arrest Narendra Kumar, had returned empty-handed. They couldn't find him at his home, nor was he at his office. Furious, she shouted at them to trace him at any cost. Then, she immediately called for a meeting and changed the plan. She ordered Devraj and Ratan Singh to escort the vehicle carrying Vijay Pratap Singh. They would travel with him for the entire day. She also asked for a report on the arrest of Narendra Kumar.

In the evening, Vijay Pratap Singh arrived at the jewellery showroom for the inauguration. The owner had organised a grand event with a celebration. He insisted that Vijay Pratap Singh stay longer at the party, but the minister politely declined, promising to attend next time.

Then, he headed to the exhibition, as per his scheduled programme. Upon arriving at the entrance, Devraj suddenly shouted, "Madam, beware!"

Kavita instantly became alert, drawing her revolver and positioning herself to protect the ex-minister. Her team quickly formed a protective shield around him. Devraj and Ratan Singh subdued a man who had tried to get too close. The man, a powerful figure, shouted, "Mr Vijay Pratap Singh!"

"Keep him away and take him to the police station," Kavita ordered sharply.

It took about fifteen minutes to clear the situation. Once it was over, CO Kavita Singh remarked sarcastically, “See, you were right. The men saved you, but it was my planning that worked.”

“I am extremely sorry, I take back what I said,” Vijay Pratap Singh conceded. “And if you don’t mind, can I proceed without security from here?”

“Sir, I would not advise that. Let us do our work. We are not interfering with you, and I hope the same from you.”

“But why? The culprit has been arrested. Why must I remain a prisoner?” he asked, visibly irritated.

“Sir, he is only a suspect. It’s not confirmed yet. I cannot allow you to take such a risk,” she repeated firmly.

“So, all this drama over a suspect?” he argued.

Kavita didn’t respond further.

After the programme concluded, Vijay Pratap Singh headed out. However, Kavita soon noticed that the car was not heading home as expected.

“Sir, do you have another engagement? You didn’t mention this before,” she asked.

“I’ve just decided to go to my farmhouse. I want to spend some time there. If you wish, you can join me, or you can leave,” he said arrogantly.

“Sir, I am not a politician. I fulfil the promises I make to people,” she replied with a smile.

“I must admit, you have a good sense of humour,” he said, a slight grin forming on his face.

“Sir, I am learning from your example,” she said, and they shared a brief laugh. Vijay Pratap Singh laughed to cover his emotions, while Kavita laughed sarcastically.

They reached his farmhouse, a large property with a grand red residential building about twenty metres from the entrance. The architecture was striking, and outside the building stood a small hut, possibly for guests.

She matched his pace while walking. At the main entrance, Vijay Pratap Singh suddenly turned and stopped her with his palm. In the process, his palm brushed against her chest and pushed her back. "This is my private property. I do not need any security here," he said in an overconfident tone.

Kavita, who was extremely sensitive to physical touch, felt deeply insulted. She thought, *Did he do this intentionally?*

She instructed her officers to secure the area. With ten policemen accompanying her, she assigned them to their positions and took a seat at the entrance of the building. As she settled in, her phone rang. It was Devraj.

"Madam, we might be making a mistake. Narendra Kumar may not be the person we're looking for," he said.

"What?" she responded sharply. "How can you say that?"

"Madam, Narendra Kumar has provided valid, consistent answers that match our facts."

"Such as?" Kavita asked, already feeling uneasy.

"He mentioned that his daughter's school is in that area. Although he couldn't recall the exact date, he believes he might have attended a parent-teacher meeting the day Nitin and Ajay were kidnapped," Devraj explained.

"Have you confirmed this?" she asked anxiously.

"Madam, we can only confirm it tomorrow, but I don't think he would lie about something like this."

"And what about his anger towards Mr Vijay Pratap Singh?"

"He says it was not anger but gratitude. The police failed to solve his wife's case, and it was only when Mr Vijay Pratap Singh intervened that he got justice. Vijay Pratap Singh helped him get reinstated after he was terminated on corruption charges," he answered.

"And why did he show up at the exhibition during the inauguration ceremony?" she pressed further.

"Madam, he said that Mr Vijay Pratap Singh's personal assistant called him and asked him to meet at the exhibition gate."

"Did he not question why a minister would call him to an event?" she asked, suspicious.

"We did ask him. He said the PA explained that Mr Vijay Pratap Singh was going to give a press briefing on the deteriorating condition of the law and wanted him to be there to share his experience," he replied.

"Have you confirmed this with the PA? As far as I know, there was no scheduled press briefing, and it never happened," she said, growing more concerned.

"Give me a minute, madam. I will check."

"Run, Devraj ji! I didn't expect this carelessness from you," she nearly shouted in frustration.

Five minutes later, Devraj returned to the call. "Madam, the PA's phone is switched off," he reported.

"What? Devraj ji, this is serious. The killer may have played his hand," Kavita said, her voice filled with alarm. She paused for a moment, and then instructed,

"Devraj ji, come to the location I'm sending you with Ratan Singh ji. Take all available staff with you."

"Madam, isn't he at his home?" Devraj asked.

"This fool has changed his plans at the last minute and gone to his farmhouse!" Kavita cried, both angry and anxious. She tried to enter the main building, but the guard at the gate stopped her. "Idiot! I must meet him immediately. He's in danger!" she shouted, but the guard refused her entry.

That was the last straw. Kavita lost her temper. She called her men and ordered them to break the door down.

The guard pointed his gun at her. Without hesitation, Kavita drew her revolver, and her officers followed suit, pointing their weapons at the guard. Other security personnel gathered around, tense and ready for a confrontation. The situation was volatile; one wrong move, and gunfire could break out.

Understanding the risk, Kavita lowered her gun and tried to reason with the head of security. "Mr Vijay Pratap Singh is in danger. Please, let us through."

Just then, she heard an engine start outside the farmhouse. She hesitated for a moment, and then shouted, "Singh! See who that is!"

Singh rushed to the gates, and Kavita, frustrated, shouted at the guard again, "Idiot, are you guarding your boss's dead body? Open the gate, now!"

It worked. The guard reluctantly opened the door, and Kavita rushed inside. Her officers and the bodyguards followed her.

They searched the entire building but found no sign of Vijay Pratap Singh. Panicking, Kavita ran to the gate, only to find Singh lying unconscious. She immediately recognised the chemical spray in the air.

"What happened, Singh? Who was in the car?" she asked, kneeling beside him.

Singh could only raise his finger to indicate the direction before collapsing. Kavita quickly instructed one constable to administer first aid to Singh and alert an ambulance. She sent another constable to fetch a car and drive in the direction Singh had pointed. Meanwhile, she radioed in to block the road and prepare for an arrest.

As she followed the car, she realised there was no other vehicle on the road. It seemed the car she was following had already gone too far. She reached a junction with three possible roads, and after a brief moment of consideration, she directed the driver to take one of them.

She continued to give instructions to her staff as they moved forward. The road narrowed, winding with several sharp turns, and fields stretched out on both sides. Suddenly, her eyes caught sight of a car parked to the side.

"Stop the vehicle here," she instructed the driver, her voice sharp with urgency. She quickly drew her revolver and stepped out, cautiously approaching the parked car. She inspected it thoroughly, but to her surprise, it was empty.

Turning to the constable, she said, "Follow me, but be quiet."

They made their way silently into the field, walking approximately fifty metres. As they proceeded, the only sound was the rustling of the grass in the breeze. Then, out of nowhere, Kavita heard a faint noise behind her. She turned instinctively, but it was too late.

A sharp, pungent chemical spray hit them both. The scent was overwhelming, and Kavita struggled to keep her composure as the world around her began to spin. She looked down and saw the constable collapsing, his body crumpling to the ground.

***

The police force arrived at the field, the same location where CO Kavita Singh had previously been. A massive spotlight illuminated the entire area as officers began their search operation. The air was thick with anticipation. Soon, they found the constable, unconscious, lying in the field. The troop leader quickly raised the alarm.

The search grew more frantic. Suddenly, the sharp sound of a gunshot pierced the still night air. Everyone sprinted towards the source of the noise, reaching the location in seconds. There, they found CO Kavita Singh standing still, almost statue-like, her revolver in hand. A man was sprawled before her, gravely injured, struggling to take his last breaths.

A female inspector stepped forward, saluting her, which snapped Kavita back into focus. With a deep breath, she regained her composure. "Call an ambulance," she ordered, her voice steady despite the gravity of the situation. "Recover Mr Vijay Pratap Singh from the field. He's 100 metres out."

A police officer found Vijay Pratap Singh lying unconscious, the cuts on his body consistent with the pattern of a skilled attacker. There were deep gashes on his thigh and wrist, severing prominent veins.

Blood was pooled around him, and his vital signs were rapidly fading.

The officers began their investigation. The scene was quickly sealed off and barricaded. The ambulance arrived, but despite their best efforts, the doctor declared the man who had been shot in the encounter dead on the spot. Vijay Pratap Singh, still alive, was rushed for immediate medical treatment.

It was 3 a.m. when the news broke. Reporters, tipped off by their sources in the police, swarmed the area. Within thirty minutes, the incident was being broadcast as breaking news across every channel. Each station rushed to cover the story, driven by the race for exclusive information.

The media was split: some channels, aligned with the opposition, focused on the failure of the state's law enforcement and administration. They raised several questions, some legitimate, others more politically motivated. Meanwhile, government-affiliated channels hailed the police response as a success, praising their swift actions.

Back at the hospital, despite every effort, Vijay Pratap Singh succumbed to his injuries. The significant blood loss had left his major organs and brain starved of oxygen, leading to multiple organ failure. Doctors worked tirelessly, but he passed away after two days of struggling between life and death.

The police took custody of his body and sent it for a postmortem. Given his prominence, the autopsy was prioritised, and the body was quickly returned to his family. The state performed the funeral with full honours, as politicians, party workers, and other leaders gathered to pay their respects. The chief minister of the state also visited to offer his condolences.

In the wake of his death, the state government called for an official inquiry to investigate the events surrounding the murder. Kavita Singh was summoned to present her side of the story. She provided all the documents detailing her actions, as well as video evidence from CCTV footage showing Vijay Pratap Singh's refusal to follow her instructions.

Just as the inquiry was progressing, an unexpected turn of events occurred. Mr Vijay Pratap Singh's widow held a press conference. She thanked the police department for their tireless efforts to save her husband. She spoke with deep emotion, stating that had her husband followed the police's instructions, he might have survived. "My husband chose to serve his people over his own life," she said, her voice cracking. "He sacrificed his life to ensure that no obstacles would come between him and the people he had vowed to serve."

After Mrs Vijay Pratap Singh's public statement, the state leadership and other critics had no grounds left to question the police. The documentary evidence, video proof, and her endorsement were enough to validate the investigation and the actions of Circle Officer Kavita Singh. The inquiry committee found no loopholes and wrote the same in their final report. They even recommended recognition for her outstanding service.

Later, Kavita, along with Devraj and Ratan Singh, was called to the superintendent's office. He stood up as they entered, his face bright with approval. "Congratulations, Kavita ji!" he said warmly. "I've recommended your name for the President's Medal."

Kavita smiled humbly. "Sir, if anyone deserves recognition, it's these two gentlemen. They worked tirelessly to crack the case. I was just fortunate enough to be there when needed."

The superintendent nodded appreciatively. "Impressive, Kavita ji. You've shown true leadership. I'll recommend their names too."

After exchanging a few more words, she took her leave and headed to her office. Ratan Singh had another investigation pending and asked for permission to depart. Once he left, Devraj asked if he could accompany her. She simply nodded, still lost deep in thought. Sensing her mood, Devraj stayed silent throughout the short journey.

Upon reaching her office, she rang the bell and ordered two teas. Then, turning to Devraj, she said, "Ask. Whatever you've been holding back."

Devraj looked startled. "How did you know I wanted to ask something?"

She smiled. "Go ahead."

He hesitated, choosing his words carefully. "Madam... did you miss the chance to save him, or...?" He left the sentence unfinished, unsure how to proceed.

Kavita leaned back slightly and said, "Devraj ji, I did what I believed was right."

"But madam," Devraj ventured again, "you were there for at least two and a half hours..."

She chuckled softly and shook her head. "There can be many theories, many versions of what might have been done differently. But how can I answer them all?" She paused, then added seriously, "Believe me, Devraj ji, I did only what was right at that moment."

"Madam, I didn't mean to doubt you," he said quickly.

"You have every right to ask," she reassured him. "You did the hard work. You have earned the right to question. But trust me, I acted with complete honesty and responsibility."

A few days later, the superintendent called a press briefing to officially close the case. Facing the press, he said firmly, "The murderer was an eccentric. He was frustrated with the investigation into the blackmailing case and wrongly suspected Ajay, Mr Vijay Pratap Singh's nephew, of being involved. This personal grudge led to his actions."

A reporter asked, "Sir, was there any evidence linking Ajay to the blackmailing?"

The superintendent replied flatly, "No."

The reporter pressed on, "Then why did the killer choose him?"

The superintendent's response was evasive: "Our investigation has found no involvement of Ajay, but we're still looking into it. We'll update you as soon as we have something."

The answer seemed unconvincing.

Another reporter, more probing, asked, "Sir, do you think the police could have done more to save Mr Vijay Pratap Singh?"

The superintendent's face tightened. "Where do you people come up with these questions? A full inquiry has already been conducted. The committee found no fault with the police. Even Mr Vijay Pratap's family has acknowledged our efforts." His voice was sharp, almost cutting. With that, he abruptly ended the briefing.

Reporters mumbled among themselves, some irritated, some moving towards the tea and snacks arranged nearby.

The superintendent returned to his room where CO Kavita Singh, Devraj, and Ratan Singh were waiting. Still muttering angrily under his breath about the reporters, he entered with a mix of laughter and frustration. Seeing him, Kavita smiled. He laughed too, a half-defeated, half-amused sound. He turned to her and said, "Kavita ji, I think you should personally meet Mrs Vijay Pratap Singh. Thank her for her support and offer our condolences."

"Of course, sir," she said, standing straight.

Then, addressing Ratan Singh and Devraj, he added warmly, "Good work, gentlemen. Keep it up. We need officers like you."

XVII

September 2023

CO Kavita Singh's car halted at the entrance of Mr Vijay Pratap Singh's house. It had been twenty days since her last visit, but the atmosphere had changed drastically. The sprawling veranda, once teeming with people, now stood empty and desolate.

She crossed the porch and reached the main building. A servant came running to her, his face tense with suspicion.

"I am CO Kavita Singh," she said, understanding his concern. "I would like to meet Mrs Vijay Pratap Singh. Is she home?"

"Please come in, madam," he replied, ushering her into the main lobby. "Kindly be seated. I'll inform madam. Would you like some water or tea?" he asked politely.

Kavita noticed the change immediately. On her previous visit, the servants had been more arrogant than their masters. Now, they were humble, almost deferential. She allowed herself a small smile at the irony.

Just then, a woman entered, a graceful, fit figure in her thirties, clad in a simple white saree. There was no need for introductions; her dignity and attire confirmed she was Mrs Vijay Pratap Singh.

Kavita rose to greet her. Mrs Singh gestured towards the couch. “Please, sit,” she said warmly. Then she turned and instructed the servant to bring tea and snacks.

“Please, madam, no formalities,” Kavita said politely.

Still, within moments, the servant returned with a tray heaped with tea and light refreshments.

“Please have some tea,” Mrs Singh offered, her voice calm but laden with sadness.

“I’ve come to pay my sincere condolences for your loss,” Kavita said, her tone equally solemn. “I tried my best to save your husband.”

“I know,” Mrs Singh replied, her voice steady. “You put your life in danger for him. I just want to say thank you.”

“Perhaps,” Kavita said hesitantly, “if your husband had followed my instructions, he might still be with us.”

Mrs Singh leaned forward, her eyes glinting. “Madam, I say this from the depths of my heart: I have no grievance against you. The killer left you no chance. You faced him bravely. You were knocked unconscious; what more could you have done?” She patted Kavita lightly on the back, almost affectionately.

Kavita studied her for a moment, and then asked carefully, “Madam, may I ask you something?”

"Oh, certainly," Mrs Singh replied.

"You mentioned the killer knocked me and my constable unconscious," Kavita said, watching her closely. "I have never disclosed that detail to anyone. How did you know?"

For a fleeting second, a shadow crossed Mrs Singh's face. She composed herself quickly and called out to the servant, "Send tea to the terrace and ask Dulari to bring it." Turning to Kavita, she smiled. "Come, let's have another cup of tea upstairs."

Kavita followed her in silence. They climbed to the highest terrace, a domed structure reminiscent of the old royal *havelis*. The climb was steep, the air thinner at the top.

Once there, Mrs Singh began speaking, her voice more secretive.

"My husband belonged to royalty. His ancestors ruled Kitnoor, near Kanpur, in British India. After the abolition of the privy purse in 1971, his father entered politics. He defeated a Congress candidate, and when Mrs Indira Gandhi invited him to contest elections after the Emergency, he won with an overwhelming margin. For the last forty-six years, my husband's family has ruled this region, not just politically, but emotionally. The people here still see them as their kings."

Dulari, a young girl of about eighteen, appeared with tea. Mrs Singh instructed her to serve and wait aside. Then, turning to Kavita again, she said with a pointed look, "You must understand why I'm telling you this. Imagine if the public found out that a respected police officer let their beloved leader die; what would happen?" She locked eyes with Kavita.

"Are you trying to scare me?" Kavita laughed lightly, not missing the veiled threat.

"No," Mrs Singh replied calmly. "We are travellers in the same boat now."

"Unfortunately, I disagree," Kavita said firmly. "I acted out of duty, without greed, without seeking personal profit."

"And you think I act out of greed or profit?" Mrs Singh asked sharply.

"Maybe for property, maybe for political gain, how would I know?" Kavita said, her voice even.

Mrs Singh smiled, almost proudly. "I already own everything here. Who could challenge me?"

"As far as I know," Kavita said, narrowing her eyes, "you are the second wife. What if the first wife comes forward to claim her share?"

Mrs Singh laughed, genuinely amused. "Impressive, CO Sahiba. You've done your homework."

"Don't forget," Kavita said coolly, "I'm a police officer. It's my job."

"But your research missed something," Mrs Singh said, sipping her tea. "I was the one who protected Vijay Pratap's first wife. Hid her safely for years. I am the reason she's alive."

"Madam," Kavita said, setting down her cup, "we could argue all day. But my question remains, were you involved in his murder?"

Mrs Singh smiled thinly. "I could ask you the same: why did you allow it to happen?"

Kavita laughed bitterly, her mind flashing back to that chaotic, blood-soaked night. Her conscience knew the truth, but the world, she realised, would always want more than just the truth.

***

She had been following the car relentlessly, but now, there was no sign of it on the deserted road. Perhaps the vehicle had sped far ahead.

Kavita Singh's vehicle reached a junction where three narrow streets diverged. She paused for a few seconds to assess the situation and then instructed the driver to take one of the roads.

The farther they went, the narrower the road became, twisting sharply through fields on either side. The countryside loomed heavy and silent.

Suddenly, she spotted the car parked off the road.

"Stop the vehicle!" she ordered sharply.

Kavita pulled out her revolver as she approached the car, signalling the constable to stay close. Carefully, she inspected the abandoned vehicle. It was empty.

Without wasting time, she gestured for the constable to follow her into the nearby fields. They moved stealthily through the thick growth, covering nearly fifty metres, when a faint noise behind her made her spin around, too late.

A sharp, pungent spray hit her senses. She glimpsed the constable collapsing to the ground before dizziness overtook her. Darkness swallowed her.

When she awoke, her hands and feet were tightly bound with rope. A thick tape was plastered across her mouth, muffling any cries. Panic threatened to rise, but she forced herself to stay calm. She scanned her surroundings.

A few metres away, she spotted Vijay Pratap Singh also bound and unconscious.

Her heart hammered against her ribs. She had faced dangerous situations before, but this was different. There was no backup, no clear plan, just helplessness.

From the shadows of the field, a masked figure emerged. His face was covered, and he carried a saw blade in his hand. He crouched down in front of her, his movements deliberate.

He reached for her face. Instinctively, she pulled back.

He chuckled softly and said, "No need to fear. I am not like this animal," jerking his thumb towards Vijay Pratap Singh. "I'm going to remove your tape. Please don't scream."

Carefully, he peeled the tape off her mouth.

"Would you like some water?" he asked with a strange politeness.

She nodded cautiously. He poured water from a bottle into a glass and brought it to her lips, letting her drink.

"If you prefer, I can make you sit more comfortably," he offered.

When she didn't respond, he interpreted her silence as consent. He lifted her and adjusted her position so she could sit.

"Listen," she began urgently. "I understand your anger. I promise you, justice can still be served. Please, let him go."

The man laughed: a cold, hollow sound.

"You don't have to worry about justice," he said. "I've already delivered it. Only he remains. Tonight, I'll rid the Earth of this filth."

"You're wrong," she pleaded. "You think you're doing the right thing, but this is murder. You can't take the law into your own hands."

He leaned back on his heels, almost amused.

"Crime?" he sneered. "Let me tell you about crime, madam. Peeping into someone's privacy is a crime. Betraying someone's trust is a crime. Forcing someone against their will is a crime. And this scoundrel," he pointed again at Vijay Pratap Singh, "is guilty of all these crimes."

"I agree with your anger," Kavita said carefully, trying to stall for time. "But you can't kill every corrupt politician."

"Ah, but this isn't just killing," he said lightly. "This is tyrannicide, a service to society."

He spoke so calmly, so confidently, that it sent chills down her spine.

Kavita knew she had to keep him talking. Every second of delay could be another second closer to rescue.

"But how do you justify calling it tyrannicide?" she challenged. "Being corrupt doesn't justify a death sentence."

He laughed again. "Madam, I have immense respect for you. You're a smart officer. But your tricks won't work. I know this area inside out. Your team can't find me here. I can hide in these fields for days. And I want him," he glared at Vijay Pratap, "to suffer, to feel the fear of death gnawing at him every second before he dies."

"Why such hatred?" Kavita pressed gently. She worked her wrists against the ropes behind her, feeling them loosen. She needed more time.

"Because," he said bitterly, "this man stole the one person I loved most."

"You're wrong," she said quickly. "You've already punished the real culprit. Vijay Pratap Singh may have abused his power, but he isn't a murderer."

He stared at her coldly. "And who told you that? Some official report? Some staged investigation?"

"I know," she stated firmly.

"How do you know?" he pressed.

"He's a responsible leader, a minister."

"Ha!" he barked a laugh. "Since when did being a minister become a certificate of innocence?"

"I believe in the investigation reports," she insisted.

He shook his head. "You believe in lies. I saw it with my own eyes. I am the eyewitness of his crime. No matter who says otherwise, the truth remains unchanged."

"Such hatred," she said softly, watching him closely. "What did he do to you?" As she spoke, she twisted her wrists harder. The knots were loosening. She needed just a few more minutes.

He leaned closer, his voice dropping to a dangerous whisper.

"He raped and murdered the woman I loved," he said, venom dripping from every word. "I saw him do it."

"You're lying!" she snapped, more out of strategy than belief.

"Believe what you want," he shrugged coldly. "The truth stands, whether you acknowledge it or not."

"Tell me," she said, feigning curiosity. "Tell me exactly what you saw."

The man's face twisted with pain and rage as memories resurfaced. He didn't realise that while he was preparing to relive his trauma, Kavita was preparing for her escape.

XVIII

July 2016

Mini reached the place at the agreed time. Upon arrival, she learnt that Shirish had booked a hotel room.

"Why did you do this, Shirish? We could have met at a park," she said, frowning.

"A park isn't safe. What if someone saw us? You could regret it later. I don't want you to regret this meeting, ever," he explained.

Although Mini wasn't fully convinced, deep down, a part of her also didn't mind staying.

Reluctantly, she entered the room with Shirish. They stayed together for more than two hours. When she left, she felt an overwhelming mix of happiness and guilt, a strange emotional cocktail. That evening, she sent Shirish a heart emoji, a silent confession of her feelings.

A few days later, Shirish wanted to meet again. Mini suggested the same hotel. It became an addiction for him, and she couldn't resist him either. Once again, they met.

However, this time, the feeling was different. Though satisfied outwardly, Mini left with a heavy heart. She reached home late. Her husband was waiting for her outside, and her daughters were hungry. Guilt gnawed at her.

That night, as she checked her phone, she found countless messages from Shirish, heart emojis, love notes. She replied with a simple but painful message: *Shirish, I love you. I know you love me too. But I humbly request you to respect my decision. I cannot continue this relationship. I hope you understand.*

Shirish was devastated. He couldn't comprehend the sudden change. He pleaded to meet her, but Mini refused and stopped responding to his calls and texts. Shirish's obsession grew. His constant messages scared Mini.

Eventually, she agreed to meet him to end things properly. In the meeting, Shirish tried desperately to convince her. Mini calmly explained her reasons. When he realised she wouldn't change her mind, he warned her ominously that he wouldn't let her go so easily.

Some days passed. Shirish kept sending messages to Mini on WhatsApp—long texts, short ones, love notes, pleading emojis—but this time, she stayed firm. She didn't reply, no matter how many times he messaged her.

Then, one evening, everything changed. She received a message from an unknown number. Curious, she opened it and froze.

It was a video. Her nude video. Captured in secret, showing her with Shirish.

Her hands trembled. Her breath caught. She forgot what it meant to sleep, what it meant to eat. Her mind shut down under the weight of humiliation and disbelief. She had never imagined Shirish would stoop so low. She had trusted him. She had loved him.

Tears filled her eyes. She didn't know what to do, whom to tell, where to hide. She was trapped inside a nightmare she couldn't wake up from.

A new message popped up on WhatsApp. It was from Shirish. He was asking her to meet him.

She had no strength left to resist. She thought he had sent the video to blackmail her, to force her to come back. She believed he was behind this cruelty. She felt betrayed, wounded beyond repair.

Crushed and broken inside, she agreed to meet him.

Entering the same hotel room, without a word, Mini began undressing.

Shirish, stunned, stopped her. "What are you doing?" he asked, confused.

"You want only this, right? Finish it quickly. My family is waiting at home," she said coldly.

"Why are you saying this? I love you! It's not just about this," he said sadly, covering her with a towel.

She pushed it away. "You're blackmailing me with that video. So, do what you want. I'll learn to act like a prostitute if needed," she said, tears streaming down her cheeks.

"What? Blackmailing you?" Shirish was horrified. "I swear on everything, I didn't shoot any video!"

"Then who sent it?" she challenged, showing him the clip.

Examining it, he said, "This isn't even my number."

He watched the video closely and noticed something. "Look carefully, this is the same room where we met last time. See that stool in the corner?"

Mini looked closer. "It means..."

"It means this room has a hidden camera!" he said, his eyes blazing. He inspected the wall, pulled aside a decorative panel, and there it was: a hidden camera.

Mini gasped and hastily dressed. "What now, Shirish? I'm scared," she whispered.

"Come with me. The manager will pay for this!" he growled, furious.

They stormed towards the reception. But as they approached, a group of bodybuilder-like men emerged, blocking their path.

"Let's go, Shirish!" Mini said, panic rising in her voice.

They came out of the hotel and stood near a small tea stall. Both ordered two cups of tea, but neither could bring themselves to drink it. Shirish wanted to say something—to offer comfort, an apology, anything—but no words came.

Suddenly, Mini's phone beeped. Another message.

She checked it and froze. It was another video. This time, it showed her undressing, recorded just an hour ago by the hidden camera in the hotel room.

Tears welled up in her eyes. She sighed heavily, broken, and said, "This will ruin my family, Shirish..."

"It's my fault, Mini! I'll fix this. Please believe me! I'll do whatever it takes to save you." Shirish's voice shook with guilt.

"How? What can you possibly do?" she said, almost whispering, her face pale and blank.

"Believe me, I'll save you," Shirish repeated, but even he had no idea how. He just wanted to ease her pain, even if it was only with hollow words.

Mini wiped her tears and said, "Can you do one last favour for me?"

"Anything."

"Please... don't try to contact me again."

Shirish couldn't say anything. He watched helplessly as she walked away, defeated and broken.

Mini had no escape left. In her heart, there was only one last fragile hope: her husband. She believed he was strong enough to handle any disaster. She decided to tell him the truth, no matter the consequences. She was ready to face whatever punishment came, trusting that somehow, he would save her.

But when she reached home, she saw her husband standing at the gate, looking furious. It was unusual; he was hardly ever home, even on holidays. Fear gripped her heart.

Had he already found out about the videos?

"What's wrong? You're at home?" she asked, trying to keep her voice steady.

"I believe this is still my house. I can come whenever I want," he snapped. His irritation was clear. "And you? Where were you? You're out of the house far too often these days!"

"One of my friends was in the hospital. I went to see her," she lied, her voice trembling.

But he wasn't listening any more. His phone rang, and he began shouting into it. From his words, she pieced together the devastating truth: he had been caught accepting a bribe, red-handed. He had been suspended pending investigation.

The ground slipped beneath her feet. Her last hope crumbled. Now, she couldn't tell him anything about her own crisis.

In the evening, another message arrived on her phone. It was an address, and a chilling instruction: *Come here alone.*

Mini felt like a fish trapped in a net. She had nowhere to run. Desperately, she thought of Shirish. He had promised to save her.

With trembling hands, she called him and explained everything.

"I know a police officer. I'll meet him right now. He might be able to help us," Shirish said, trying to sound confident.

"Will he really help? Please, Shirish... save me," she begged, breaking into sobs.

"Don't cry! I swear, Mini, nobody will touch you as long as I'm alive." His voice was firm, determined.

For the first time in days, she felt a flicker of hope.

Shirish rushed to the police station and requested to meet the in-charge. But when the officer called him inside, Shirish found it difficult to explain.

The inspector, a middle-aged man with a heavy moustache, gave him an encouraging look and said, "Come on, young man. No one comes here without a problem. Tell me everything."

"Sir... someone's blackmailing us," Shirish said hesitantly.

The officer smirked. "Us? Who's 'us?' If I'm guessing right, it's your girlfriend?"

"Yes, sir," Shirish confessed, feeling ashamed.

He described the blackmailing, stumbling over words, ashamed of every detail.

The in-charge listened silently. After a long pause, he said, "We'll take strict action. But for that, I need a written complaint."

Shirish hesitated. Fear gripped him. But the officer insisted, "No complaint, no action."

Finally, Shirish wrote everything down and handed it over.

The inspector read it carefully, stopping at a certain line. "You're sure about the name of the hotel you've written here?" he asked.

"Yes, sir. Look, here's the receipt," Shirish said, showing it.

The officer glanced at the bill and then gave a crooked smile. "You know who owns that hotel?" he asked.

"No, sir... who?"

"Mr Vijay Pratap Singh's nephew."

Hearing the name sent a chill down Shirish's spine. Vijay Pratap Singh was a powerful, feared man in the city, the home minister of the state.

"If he hears about this complaint, he won't let you stay alive," the officer said coldly. "I suggest you remove the hotel's name from your complaint."

"But sir, if I remove it, what will you even investigate?! He's the one responsible!" Shirish protested.

"Give me the receipt again," the officer said, extending his hand.

As soon as Shirish handed it over, the officer tore it in half and tossed it into the dustbin.

"What are you doing, sir? That was my only proof!" Shirish shouted, shocked.

"Shut your mouth!" the officer barked and shoved him lightly.

"Sir… I came here with hope… and you're helping them!" Shirish said bitterly, fighting the lump in his throat.

The officer leaned closer and growled, "You said you received a message? Show it to me."

"I do not have the message; my friend received the message."

The officer laughed. "Then send her to lodge the complaint."

"Sir, she cannot come here. Please understand, sir!"

"She can go with you to a hotel room, but she cannot come here?" he taunted.

"Sir, she is a respected woman. Please do not use abusive words with her," Shirish said arrogantly.

"Respected woman, my foot! I know these types of women. Such a cheap woman could cheat anyone if she can cheat on her husband. Bloody call girl!" he exclaimed rudely in an insulting tone.

"Sir, please don't talk like this. Please help us. Where will we go if you don't help us?"

"Get out and run! Never come here again. Rascal! Ram Singh, throw him out!" he shouted at him.

Shirish felt helpless. He wanted to slap the in-charge, but could not. The uniform he wore had power which he could not fight. He came out of the police station and sat in front of a shop, helpless. His phone rang. It was Mini.

"Shirish, did you go to the police station?" she asked.

"Yes! But how do you know this? I just came out of the police station," he said, astonished.

"Is this your plan to save me? Oh, Shirish! How could I be such a fool?" she said with disappointment.

"Mini, I thought the police would help us in this situation." Shirish was also disappointed.

"Do you know what they did? They informed the blackmailer, and he called me to his place." She was almost weeping.

"I will not leave you alone with this problem. I will go with you," he said in a firm voice.

"You cannot come with me. These rascals have called me alone, and if I don't go, they will come to my house. I've made a big mistake, but I cannot let my family get in trouble." She was determined.

"Mini, it is dangerous to go there alone. Please let me come with y—"

Mini did not let him complete his sentence and disconnected the phone.

Shirish understood that Mini was going to make a big mistake. It could be the start of endless blackmailing.

He decided to save her from this. He reached her home on his bike and waited for her to leave.

Around 5 p.m., she came out of her home and went to the market. Shirish started following her. Mini roamed in the market till 7.30 p.m. He understood that she was passing the time there. It was a dangerous sign; the blackmailer had called her at night, and it was self-explanatory.

Shirish also made some purchases: a knife, a pepper spray bottle, and an iron chain. At around 7.45 p.m., she reached an empty bus stand, which had been out of use for a long time. She waited there for a few minutes until a van stopped near her. She entered the van.

Shirish started following the van, which took him to a school on the city's outskirts. The van left her and turned back. She was alone in that place. Shirish went up to her.

"Shirish!" She was astonished to see him. "Why did you come here? Please go, for God's sake. These people will not let you live."

"I do not care, Mini. I will not leave you alone here in danger," he said firmly.

"Shirish, swear to me that you will not stay here any longer," she said and entered the school.

Shirish kept standing like a statue.

He swore to her but decided not to leave, choosing instead to wait for the blackmailer. He decided to kill the blackmailer to save her from defamation. Soon, an SUV arrived, and four bodybuilders got out. Shirish had expected two or a maximum of three people, but these four were out of his capacity. He was questioning his courage to take them on in a fight when suddenly, another SUV arrived with five more people.

He was shocked to see the person exiting the latter SUV. He was the home minister of the state, Vijay Pratap Singh. The other four were his bodyguards. He asked one of the men who had come earlier, "Where is she?"

"She is on the school premises and waiting for you," he replied laughingly.

Vijay Pratap Singh laughed in reply too.

Shirish could not believe what his eyes saw. His entire body froze with terror. He stood there, paralysed, unable to gather the courage to move.

One by one, the men entered the school building, while four bodyguards remained posted outside like silent statues.

Moments later, a blood-curdling scream tore through the darkness. Mini's cry of pain shattered whatever was left of Shirish's spirit.

He cursed himself bitterly for his cowardice. Each scream from inside ripped apart his dignity, crushed his self-respect, and humiliated his very existence. He clenched his fists, wanting to run in, but fear wrapped its cold hands around his throat. He couldn't move.

The horrifying sounds of Mini's agony continued for what felt like an eternity. Two hours. Two brutal hours of helplessness.

Eventually, her voice grew fainter, until even her pain surrendered to exhaustion.

Shirish stood still, like a dead tree rooted in shame. Vijay Pratap Singh was the first to exit, laughing, surrounded by his cohorts. One by one, the other men followed, cracking jokes about Mini and mocking her screams. The last man to leave joined the group, basking in the praise for some perceived act of heroism. The bodyguards lingered a while longer, smoking cigarettes, talking casually, and then left the area as if nothing had happened.

Silence returned to the ruined school ground. The night air felt heavier, suffocating.

Shirish remained there, broken, until he lost his senses.

It was only when he saw Mini staggering out of the building that he snapped back to life. She moved unsteadily, her steps weak, like a shattered doll. She was completely naked, blood streaming down her thighs.

Seeing her like this, Shirish's heart broke into a thousand pieces. He ran towards her.

When he touched her arm to support her, she screamed in terror.

"It's me, Mini! It's me!" Shirish wept aloud, his voice shaking.

"Shirish... you?" Mini whispered faintly, barely conscious. "Can you... can you give me some water?"

"Wait! I'll bring it!"

He rushed to find a vessel, anything, but there was nothing around. Desperate, he scooped water from the hand pump with his bare hands and let her sip from his cupped palms.

She drank a little and slumped back again. Tears streamed down Shirish's face. He couldn't stop them any more.

She looked at him with hollow eyes.

"Why did you stay, Shirish? They could have killed you..." she whispered painfully.

"I have already died tonight, Mini," he said, sobbing. "I am a coward... not worthy of living."

Mini tried to smile but failed. "See, Shirish... this is the price I paid... for loving you."

"Wait here, I'll find your clothes. I'll take you to a hospital," he said desperately and ran towards the classrooms.

But he found nothing, no clothes, no hope. When he returned, Mini looked even weaker, death brushing her cheeks.

As he turned to run again, she grabbed his hand weakly.

"You never listened to me, Shirish," she whispered, struggling for every breath. "At least listen now... These monsters... they need a scapegoat. I don't want you to be the next. Please... please leave..."

"I can't!" he cried. "I can arrange something, anything! We have to save you!"

"Go!" she said sharply this time. "I cannot go to any hospital with you. I bore all this... to save my family's name. Don't make my sacrifice meaningless."

Shirish collapsed to his knees, helpless. He cried like a child, loud, raw, broken.

"You paid the price for loving me. Now it's my turn," he said finally, his voice choking.

He stood up, one last look at her bruised, bleeding body burning into his soul. He took a step back and froze, unable to move further.

Mini, barely conscious, opened her swollen eyes one last time and smiled faintly at him, a broken, tragic smile filled with pain, love, and a silent farewell. Her trembling lips moved, forming words he could barely hear:

"Go... please... before they come back..."

At that moment, headlights flashed in the distance. The rumble of engines echoed across the empty ground.

Panic jolted through Shirish. More of Vijay Pratap's men were returning, maybe to clean up their crime. If he stayed even a second longer, he would be killed. And if he died here, no one would ever know the truth. Mini's suffering would vanish into darkness, unavenged and forgotten.

Tears blurred his vision as he stared at her fragile form. She was lying near the old hand pump, her body trembling, her life slipping away. Blood stained the dusty ground around her, a silent testament to the horrors she had endured.

"Forgive me, Mini," he whispered, his voice cracking. "I will not let your sacrifice go to waste. I swear it on your pain."

With a soul heavier than stone, he forced his legs to move. Every step away from her felt like a betrayal. He didn't dare look back again because if he did, he knew he would never be able to leave.

Mini's broken smile was the last thing he carried with him into the darkness, a wound deeper than death, a memory that would haunt him forever.

***

The police declared that they had caught the culprit of the "Sabala" case. They presented the accused at a press briefing. He was around forty-five years old. The police described his crime, claiming that he had kidnapped her from a bus stand.

Shirish had been watching the news since morning. He immediately recognised the police inspector: the same man he had once approached for help. He understood then: the investigation would never be fair. Determined to do something, he decided to meet Mini's husband. When he reached their home, he found the entire street crowded with people. Upon enquiry, he learnt that the state home minister, Mr Vijay Pratap, was expected shortly.

The minister arrived to offer his condolences, but his words were a hollow mockery of justice. At the press conference, he announced that a fast-track court would be set up for the case proceedings. He added, almost gleefully, that all previous corruption charges against Mini's husband had been dropped, giving him "another chance at life".

Shirish felt his world collapse. The truth was unmistakable now: the powerful minister had bought the victim's family, and with it, his last hope for a fair trial. The walls were closing in on him.

Yet, he didn't know what exactly to do. For three years, Shirish was consumed by an internal war, a constant battle between his cowardice and his guilt. Each day felt like a slow death, his heart burdened with the weight of his inaction. He stood by, helpless, frozen by the fear of facing the mighty forces that controlled everything: the powerful minister, the corrupt system, and the society that had turned a blind eye to Mini's suffering. Every time he considered speaking up, fear gripped him. He told himself it was too dangerous, too impossible. They would crush him, just as they had crushed her.

But at night, the guilt would rise. It suffocated him. Her screams echoed in his mind, relentless, a constant reminder of his failure. He could still hear her voice, begging him, as her body was torn apart by those monsters. He had promised her that he would save her, and yet he had turned away, a coward in the face of cruelty.

There were moments when the guilt felt too much to bear. He thought of his own soul, rotting under the weight of his silence. How could he ever live with himself, knowing he had abandoned her when she needed him the most? The faces of the powerful—the politicians, the officers, the untouchable criminals—mocked him from every direction. He was just one man, insignificant and weak. How could he ever fight them?

And yet, somewhere deep inside, something stirred, a flicker of defiance. He had been a coward for too long, and now the fear was no longer enough to keep him silent. The memories of Mini's pain, her trust, her last cry for help, they became the fire that slowly burned away his terror. He could feel the anger rising inside him, fighting the years of self-doubt and fear.

But still, the overwhelming weight of helplessness threatened to drag him back into the shadows. How could he possibly take on such powerful enemies? The minister, the police, the corrupt system, they had already won. He was nothing. Who would believe him? Who would stand with him?

Then came the breaking point, the moment when his guilt finally overpowered his fear. Shirish looked at Mini's photo, at her innocent smile, and for the first time in years, he understood. It was no longer about fighting the system. It was about fighting for her.

And he would do whatever it took.

He began reading all the news reports about the case. One article caught his attention: an interview with the superintendent of police regarding Sabala. The superintendent boasted that there were no loopholes in the investigation. He proudly stated that they had matched the bite marks and nail scratches found on the victim's body with the accused, and had verified all genetic evidence collected from her body.

He also praised the doctor who had conducted the postmortem. One particular sentence stuck in Shirish's mind. How could they have collected genetic evidence from a person who was never there? Shirish knew then that the doctor had either been pressured by Vijay Pratap Singh or had sold his honesty.

Determined, he began frequenting the local police station, where he identified a constable infamous for his drinking habits. Slowly, Shirish befriended him. It wasn't difficult; he simply kept buying him alcohol and winning his confidence.

He spent three long months building trust.

One night, as they drank together, Shirish casually asked, "Kanti bhai, what exactly is a postmortem?"

Kanti Lal burst out laughing. "You don't know what a postmortem is? Really?"

"Yeah! Really!" Shirish said innocently.

"When someone dies unnaturally, doctors cut open the body to find out the cause of death," Kanti explained with exaggerated gestures.

"Have you ever seen one yourself?" Shirish pressed.

"Why would I? It's not my job," Kanti shrugged.

"Then how do you know what the doctor sees?"

"You're not as big a fool as you act!" Kanti laughed loudly. "The doctor just writes observations on a predesigned format."

"Oh! What kind of a format?" Shirish feigned interest and quickly added, "The police officer handling the Sabala case is from your station, right?"

"Yes, Inspector Devendra Kumar is investigating it."

Shirish leaned forward, speaking like a child making a request. "You have to do me a favour, Kanti bhai."

"Anything for you! Tell me!" he replied happily.

"I want to see a postmortem report. Can you show me one?"

The constable made a face. "Ugh! What a weird desire! Ask for something else, I'll arrange it."

"Please! If possible, get me the Sabala case report," Shirish insisted.

"You've spoilt my mood!" Kanti grumbled.

"I'm sorry if I irritated you. I just genuinely want to see it. If you can't help, it's okay," Shirish said, changing the subject.

He was heartbroken. Three months of effort seemed wasted. The next night, Shirish ignored Kanti's calls. But Kanti kept calling him again and again. Finally, Shirish picked up.

"Where the hell are you? Why aren't you picking up my calls?" Kanti roared.

"Ah! I was busy with some work. My phone was on silent. I didn't realise you were calling," Shirish lied calmly.

"Come quickly! I'm waiting in our den," Kanti said and hung up.

Cursing under his breath, Shirish went to meet him.

"You're late! I've already started celebrating!" Kanti waved a half-full bottle at him.

Shirish smiled weakly and muttered, "The bloody drunkard!"

He pulled a chair and sat in front of him. Kanti quickly poured him a drink. Shirish sipped slowly, not expecting much.

Suddenly, Kanti cried out, "Tada! Here's something for you!" He waved a piece of paper in front of Shirish's face.

"What's this?" Shirish grabbed it.

His heart almost stopped. It was the postmortem report of the Sabala case. Shirish kissed Kanti's hand and quickly snapped a photo of the paper on his phone.

The report was full of lies, just as he had expected. But he wasn't interested in the report itself. He needed the name and address of the doctor who had signed it.

He asked Kanti for permission to leave.

"So early? Why?" Kanti complained.

"Boss, I told you I'm working on something. I have to go," Shirish replied.

"As you wish! But I still have many secrets about this case! If you don't want to know, it's your choice!" Kanti said, slurring.

"What secrets?" Shirish asked cautiously.

"Do you know... our Inspector Devendra Kumar was desperate to take over the Sabala case?" Kanti whispered.

"But it's his duty. He has to investigate such cases," Shirish said.

"He's not that kind of an officer!" Kanti laughed bitterly. "He usually dumps bodies into other jurisdictions to avoid new investigations!"

"Other jurisdictions? What do you mean?"

Kanti explained, "Jurisdiction means the boundary under a particular police station. If a dead body is found inside your area, your station must handle the case. Otherwise, you can push the responsibility elsewhere."

"Okay, so it means the place where the body was found shares its boundary with other police stations," Shirish tried to understand.

"No, dear! This place is unique in the city. It shares boundaries with five police stations. That's why it's a favourite spot for criminals. Murderers, rapists, all types of criminals find it perfect," Kanti laughed.

"Why so?" Shirish asked curiously.

"See! Not a single SHO wants to increase the crime rate in his area. So, they fight to push the case into another jurisdiction. Sometimes they even throw unknown bodies into neighbouring areas. Smart criminals take advantage of this," he explained.

"How does it share a boundary with so many stations?" Shirish asked, showing deeper curiosity.

"Why are you so interested? Planning to commit a crime?" Kanti teased.

"No, no!" Shirish replied hurriedly.

"Haha!" Kanti laughed. "I know you're a goat. You can't do anything!"

Then, Kanti explained the entire geography of the area. Shirish secretly recorded everything on his mobile. It was time to act.

He started mapping the site and marking the people involved. His first target was the doctor who had betrayed his duty by filing a false postmortem report.

Shirish began following the doctor to understand his daily routine. One day, outside the doctor's office, he spotted a man he recognised immediately. He was one of the four men Shirish had seen that night. Controlling his emotions with difficulty, he decided to follow him.

The man went inside a house, and Shirish waited outside at a tea stall. He ordered a cup of tea and struck up a conversation with the stall owner. After a few minutes of chit-chat, he got the information he needed. The man's name was Ajay, the state home minister's nephew. He owned the hotel where someone had shot that video of Mini and him. He was one of the main culprits, and by his attitude, he seemed to carry no guilt at all. They had given a painful death to an innocent woman and were now roaming free, shamelessly. Shirish vowed to make him suffer a death as painful as Mini's.

That evening, he spent hours on Facebook, piecing faces and names together. He recognised all four culprits and made a list of seven people directly or indirectly responsible for Mini's death: the doctor, the inspector, Vijay, Ajay, Nitin, Rahul, and the most disgusting of all, Vijay Pratap Singh. He ranked them carefully.

First: the doctor.

Last: Vijay Pratap Singh.

He placed Vijay Pratap at the end, because trapping him would be the toughest, with the highest chance of failure. Still, Shirish planned to kill them all, and if he failed, he swore to take down as many as he could. He could never erase from his mind the image of Mini's painful death, the heavy blood loss, the helpless waiting for death, the silent screams. That memory burned inside him, feeding his hatred, sharpening his resolve.

He decided on a method as cruel as their crime: cutting prominent veins, causing slow, agonising deaths—not instant, but full of unbearable waiting, just like Mini had suffered.

Fortunately, Shirish had once been a biology student. His old knowledge of the human anatomy and physiology, buried deep in his mind, now came back with brutal clarity. To prepare himself, Shirish secretly studied human physiology. He spent nights poring over medical textbooks and anatomy diagrams, learning about the major veins, the ones closest to the surface, the ones that, if severed, would cause heavy, unstoppable bleeding. He learnt where to strike, how deep to cut, and how death would arrive, slowly, painfully, inevitably. He would not give them the mercy of a quick end. He would make them live their last moments drowning in the fear and agony they had once inflicted.

He chose a secluded place for his first kill: the doctor. It wasn't a random choice. Shirish knew the first step was the most crucial; one mistake, and everything would collapse. He couldn't afford to fail.

As preparation, he spent several nights continuously visiting and observing the location. He studied the geography carefully: the access points, possible escape routes, blind spots, the natural cover of trees, and abandoned structures. He timed the movement of stray animals, the rare vehicles that passed by, even the shifting patterns of moonlight and darkness. He memorised every inch of that area. He trained himself to move silently in the dark, blending with the shadows.

He rehearsed his plan mentally, again and again, until it became a reflex, until fear could not unnerve him. He understood this first kill was not just revenge. It was war. And in war, precision was survival.

Although his heart boiled with hatred, when it came to execution, he hesitated. He had never killed a mouse in his life, and now he was planning to kill seven men. Once, he even thought about leaving their fate to God's justice. But the court verdict shook him deeply: Chatar Singh, the scapegoat, was sentenced to capital punishment.

That day, Shirish made a decision, one that hardened his soul forever: "If I don't stop these monsters, they'll destroy many more innocents."

He knew there would be no turning back. He sold off everything he could spare and spent all his savings to buy a second-hand car, an old, battered vehicle, perfect for staying unnoticed. He cleaned it thoroughly, removed any identification marks, and kept essential tools hidden inside: ropes, duct tape, deep-sleep sprays, a first-aid kit for himself, and extra clothes to change identities if needed.

The moment he had been preparing for finally came. It was a humid evening in August 2019 when Shirish positioned himself on the route Dr Prakash usually took to return home on foot. Hidden behind a broken wall, he waited with the patience of a predator.

When he spotted the doctor approaching, busy on his phone, careless as ever, Shirish stepped out calmly, pretending to be a lost stranger.

"Excuse me, sir," he said politely, holding out a fake address scribbled on a piece of paper, "can you help me find this place?"

At the same time, a resident of the locality stepped out of his house. He saw Dr Prakash and greeted him. Dr Prakash replied to his greeting warmly, then glanced at Shirish, arrogance dripping from his posture, and leaned in to read the note. Meanwhile, the resident approached the doctor and said, "Prakash, what are your chances for the post of principal of the medical college?"

Shirish sighed; the chance had slipped. Now, they were indulging in discussions about college politics for the post of principal. Shirish was disappointed. He took back the piece of paper, realising it was useless now. Dr Prakash was startled by this, but since he was busy talking with the man, he didn't notice.

Shirish left the colony. He had no choice but to postpone the plan. He couldn't make a second attempt soon because Prakash or that resident would identify him.

At night, he rethought the incident. Meanwhile, he got a call from his brother. His mother was seriously ill. Did destiny want to stop him? He knew his mother had made many sacrifices to raise him. In the last few months, he had forgotten that he had a family and, importantly, his mother.

His belief in his plan began to shake. He went to the hospital. His brother and his wife were sitting in the gallery. Behind him, his sister appeared. As she looked at him, she started scolding both brothers for their carelessness. His younger brother accepted his mistake, saying he was busy with his professional duties, but Shirish had nothing to say. He calmly accepted his sister's blame because she was right.

The next ten days were the busiest, as Shirish did everything to take care of his mother. He was already irregular at his job, and the senior management had issued a warning just a few days ago. Shirish had been careless about his job, but with the changing situation, he realised he needed the job as long as his mother was alive. He considered it a hint of destiny, but deep down, he knew he was trying to escape the decision he had made.

He attended a meeting and assured his bosses that he would remain regular in his service and requested for a second chance. He was a good worker and an asset to the company, so his bosses thought his mental state was disturbed due to his mother's illness and allowed him one more month for her recovery.

But the tenth day of hospitalisation proved to be a life-changing event in his life. His mother died. Shirish was numb. His brother and sister wept in front of him, but he felt relaxed. The last string was broken. The three siblings decided to cremate their mother on the banks of the holy Ganga.

During the cremation, a scuffle occurred between the attendees and some frivolous boys. Someone called the police. The sub-inspector ordered the constables to bring all the boys to the police station. One of them came forward and shouted at the sub-inspector, "Don't you know who I am? The son of Shri Ratan Lal. Mr Vijay Pratap Singh, the home minister, is our relative."

The name Vijay Pratap Singh infuriated Shirish. He came out of the crowd to teach him a lesson, but as soon as he saw the boy, that fateful night flashed through his mind. He had been the last man to leave the crime scene. The other four were laughing at his brutality, and he walked as if he had done something brave. He felt the fire of the pyre searing his soul. He saw Mini with tears in that pyre. His hands trembled with rage.

He went near the boy, who dialled the home minister's number. Shirish said, "I am extremely sorry, sir. We did not know you were the home minister's relative. Please excuse us."

That boy, Vijay, Ratan Lal's son, slapped Shirish. Shirish's brother strode towards them in rage, but Shirish calmed him and requested, "Sir, we are cremating our mother. If you allow us, we will perform the ritual."

The SI, who had looked scared when Vijay dialled the number of the home minister, requested him too. Vijay granted him permission, as if he were a king.

That was the moment Shirish changed his mind. He understood the hint of destiny: he couldn't run from his decision. He narrowed his target. It was Vijay who would become his first kill.

Gathering information about Vijay wasn't difficult, but it took two months. Kanti Lal once again proved to be a valuable resource, sharing with Shirish the details of Vijay's unregistered cases. It seemed Vijay was the spoilt son of a wealthy businessman, using his connections with a powerful politician to get away with crimes.

Shirish told Kanti about his desire to test a specific drug. Kanti laughed and said, "You are becoming a rascal day by day." And the next day, he gave him a pouch of white powder, a drug seized from an addict and a drug peddler.

Shirish had the bait, and he had to lure the fish. He followed Vijay and found him alone on a road, waiting for a taxi. A glimpse of that powder was sufficient to lure him inside the car. The spray did the rest of the work. A police van passed by his car, and a constable stepped down to check. Shirish handed him a Rs 500 note and said his friend was sleeping in the car, and that he had stopped for a smoke because he was feeling sleepy. The constable checked the sleeping man in the darkness. The smell of alcohol wafting from inside told him he had the right to keep the Rs 500 note. He abused both of them and told the inspector that everything was perfect.

The hunt had officially begun.

Taking him to the predetermined, secluded place, Shirish parked the car deep inside the grove and dragged Vijay out, tying him tightly to an old iron chair he had bolted to the ground days before.

Under the faint light of a single battery-operated lantern, Shirish splashed cold water on Vijay's face. Vijay jerked awake, disoriented, his eyes wide with terror. Before he could scream, Shirish clamped a hand over his mouth and then applied tape.

Vijay struggled to free himself but failed.

"Why are you here?" Shirish leaned in close. He held a knife in his hand and rubbed it on his shirt, as if cleaning the blade. "You rape a woman, kill her, and escape. You lynch someone at the cremation ground and threaten them because a mighty politician is in your circle. But everything has a limit. Enough is enough!"

Shirish placed his knife on Vijay's legs. It took him some time to decide where to cut. He tried, but couldn't. He again placed the knife on Vijay's thigh, but in vain. He closed his eyes and made the first incision, but it didn't satisfy him. He tried again and made a few more cuts, and finally, he got his desired incision. He repeated the same steps with Vijay's wrists, waited for some time, and then freed him. "You can run to save your life."

Vijay looked at him in disbelief, and started running. He tried to run fast, but couldn't go more than thirty or forty metres. He removed the tape over his mouth and tried to shout, but no sound came out. Shirish walked up and sat in front of him, showing him a newspaper cutting with the headline: "Woman's Naked Body Found in a School."

The next few months were chaotic. The efficient police, who had solved the Sabala case in just one month, were unable to find a clue about Vijay for the next three years. The revelation of the women's blackmailing case, the home minister Vijay Pratap's suspension, and finally the COVID-19 pandemic were the reasons that kept Shirish from acting again during that time. He did his routine job silently, got promotions, but soon realised he had turned to stone. No joy made him cheerful; no sadness hurt him. He calmly waited for the next opportunity, which came three years later when he read the news that Dr Prakash had been shortlisted for the post of principal of the medical college.

The news sparked something in him. If a person like Dr Prakash became a principal, he would create more Dr Prakashs, and Shirish was not ready for that. He set a trap against him.

He used the same old technique, asking for an address, but this time he chose the place carefully: the ground between the administrative block and the residential building. He stopped the doctor near the ground to ask about an address and, in one swift motion, sprayed the deep-sleep chemical straight on his face. The doctor stumbled, tried to shout, but no sound came. Within seconds, he slumped into unconsciousness.

Without wasting a breath, Shirish dragged his limp body into the car, tied him securely, and disappeared into the night.

It had been more than three years. Shirish hadn't practised, so he decided to ask the doctor himself. After all, he was an anatomy specialist. He whispered coldly, *"Tell me... which veins do I need to cut to cause a slow, painful death?"*

The doctor's face turned white. He stammered, "W-What do you want to do?"

"I want to kill you," Shirish said, his voice flat, almost tender in its cruelty. "But not quickly. I want you to wait for your death... just like Mini did."

Shivering uncontrollably, Dr Prakash tried to reason with him. “But... I don’t even know any Mini! Why are you doing this to me?”

Shirish showed him the same newspaper cutting, and before Prakash could say something, he cut him off sharply.

“Sabala.”

The name alone seemed to slice through the night air. Shirish’s eyes darkened further. The doctor, trembling, began pleading for mercy. Through choked sobs, he confessed, “I was under pressure... Vijay Pratap Singh... he forced me to make the false report... I had no choice...”

Shirish leaned closer, his voice now a dangerous whisper. “Your false report killed two people,” he said, “and both had to wait for death. One died bleeding on the ground; the other is still rotting in jail, waiting every day for the end.”

“Believe me, I am not dishonest, but I was under pressure.” The doctor repeated without listening to Shirish.

“The time has gone, doctor. Now, can you tell me which veins are prominent, which should I cut?” Shirish couldn’t believe that he was speaking this, with this calmness.

Terrified beyond reason, Dr Prakash, trying desperately to save his life, showed him the key points—the radial artery, the femoral vein, and the jugular—detailing how blood loss from these would cause inevitable, drawn-out death.

He nodded once, coldly, and whispered, “Thank you.”

The doctor broke down completely, but Shirish continued, his words like knives: “I didn’t even show you a weapon, and yet, you told me exactly how to kill someone slowly and painfully. Just imagine the agony of those who suffered because of your cowardice."

Though this wasn't Shirish's first kill, he was doing it after two years—a long gap, sufficient to dull anyone's practice. His hand trembled as he made the first incision. His breath was shaky, his confidence faltering. The cuts weren't as clean as he had imagined; some were wrong, too shallow, too uncertain. He hesitated, wondering if he could really go through with it. But the faces of Mini and her culprits filled his mind, and he pushed his doubts aside, forcing himself to continue. Dr Prakash screamed, a raw, animal-like sound that the isolation of the grove quickly swallowed.

The blood began to flow, and death, slow, creeping, merciless, began its dance.

Shirish sat a few feet away, silently watching as the doctor writhed in agony. After a few moments, Shirish untied the doctor's hands and legs, allowing him to get up and escape. Fearful of his impending death, the doctor scrambled to his feet and ran. But after just a few metres, he realised the bleeding had only worsened, and that the flow of blood increased with each step. He collapsed to the ground, frantically trying to stop the bleeding, but it was futile.

He pleaded for mercy, but Shirish remained deaf to his cries, unmoved by the desperation. He had ranked the doctor first for this very reason, because betrayal by someone entrusted to save lives deserved no forgiveness.

The night devoured the doctor's last cries, and Shirish rose, one step closer to the justice he had sworn to deliver.

***

Capturing Inspector Devendra Kumar was much harder, because his uniform was his armour. Shirish didn't want to leave his mission half done, so he changed the sequence. Meanwhile, Nitin and Rahul were out of the city.

In these circumstances, he set his sights on Rahul as his next target. Rahul was easy prey. But then, he got arrested in the blackmail case. With resources stretched thin, the investigation faced delays, but eventually, the court sentenced all four accused to seven years' imprisonment, removing him from Shirish's list.

Then, unexpectedly, a dacoity case broke out in the city. This gave Shirish the opportunity he needed. He tricked Inspector Devendra Kumar into meeting him alone by pretending to offer a tip about the dacoity.

For six days, Shirish kept Devendra Kumar imprisoned in a decaying forest outpost long abandoned by the world, much like justice. The musty place was a fitting prison for a man who had betrayed his oath to uphold the truth.

Each morning, Shirish fed him. Each night, he stood in the dark corridor, listening, sometimes to Devendra's sobs, sometimes to the silence that was more haunting than screams. And each day, Shirish whispered the same word: *"Tomorrow."*

Devendra, once the lion of a police department, was now reduced to a caged relic. His arrogance had rotted into fear. His words, once sharp with authority, now fumbled like a child's prayer. He begged. He reasoned. He wept.

And yet, as the days passed, Shirish's hatred faltered.

He had imagined this moment countless times, Mini's face burned into his memory, her screams echoing in his skull, but the reality was darker. Devendra didn't look like a monster any more. He looked like an old man defeated by time. His spine had curved with guilt, or perhaps cowardice. His breath rasped like someone waiting for judgement, too weak to ask for mercy.

Shirish's mind turned on itself. Was this justice? Or vengeance dressed as virtue?

He paced through the nights, staring at Mini's photo, hoping for answers from eyes long closed. His hand trembled when he unlocked the door. His conscience gnawed at him. He questioned himself in whispers and dreams. Once or twice, he nearly let Devendra go.

But then came the sixth night. Shirish entered with food. Devendra didn't lift his head.

"I haven't eaten since yesterday," he murmured. "But I won't eat tonight. I know it ends here."

His voice wasn't angry or pleading, just emptied of hope. Shirish felt a flicker of empathy, a breath away from mercy.

And then, Devendra whispered, "I was just following orders."

Shirish stopped cold. That one sentence, so familiar, so cowardly, shattered whatever mercy had survived. It wasn't a confession. It was an escape. Even now, with death in the room, Devendra wouldn't admit his fault. He hadn't changed. He still believed hiding behind the system absolved him of his sin.

Shirish's chest tightened. His vision blurred with rage. The image of Mini returned, not as memory, but as pain. Her eyes, her breathless cries, her blood on the ground.

He thought of every girl ignored, every report buried, every policeman who became a puppet of power and called it duty. Devendra wasn't sorry. He was still shielding himself with the lie of helplessness.

That was the trigger.

Something dead inside Shirish came back to life: not guilt, not doubt, just clarity. He saw Devendra not as a man, but a symbol. A system. A rot that refused to be accountable. That night, Shirish didn't argue. He didn't shout. He just left.

He didn't return until dawn.

And when he did... he didn't bring food.

***

As for Nitin and Ajay, Shirish didn't have to work too hard. He used the same method he had perfected, the drug-laced cigarette, and captured them easily.

One by one, he finished them all. All, except the biggest monster of them all:

Vijay Pratap Singh.

***

He finished telling his story to Kavita Singh. It took him a long time to explain his reasons for the killings. Kavita used this time to free her hands, and she was nearly successful in her objective. She then asked about Vijay Pratap Singh, "How did you get him?"

"A bunch of genius officers under your guidance left no stone unturned to make my job difficult, but I got help from someone in his house. Without this help, I wouldn't have been able to get this rascal," he replied with a laugh.

"Who was the person?"

"I know you're an efficient police officer, and I know you won't forget your duty even in this situation. I'm a big fan of yours," he said, almost mocking her.

Suddenly, she freed her hands and stood up, astonishing him.

He shouted, "Madam, please don't move. I don't want to hurt you, but I can't leave him alive. Please don't force me to do something wrong."

Kavita moved towards him, forcing him to step back. He lost his balance and fell. Suddenly, Vijay Pratap Singh broke free and grappled with Shirish. He was healthier than Shirish and easily overpowered him. He grabbed Shirish's knife and raised his hand to stab him.

"Mr Vijay Pratap Singh, don't!" she shouted.

"Officer, stay out of this. I'll kill him and reward you for saving me," Vijay Pratap Singh sneered. Then he turned to Shirish. "You want revenge? I'll give you your vindication, in your ass!"

"Mr Vijay Pratap, leave him, or I'll shoot you," Kavita warned.

"I can't leave him alive. He's a witness, and you can use him against me," he said rudely.

"You're admitting to what he told me?!" she exclaimed in surprise.

Vijay Pratap Singh laughed. “Does it matter? He is the only one who can tell this to the world. I’ll finish him off with that.” Instantly, he moved to stab Shirish, but failed. Kavita caught his hand.

Irritated, he stood up, saying, “Okay, as you wish. You want to die? I’ll fulfil your wish.”

“Try, if you can,” she challenged him.

Vijay Pratap Singh tried, but failed. He had forgotten that Kavita Singh was a trained officer. She may have been half his size, but she was twice as agile. In seconds, she showed him what a woman could do. Vijay Pratap Singh was on the ground, and she placed her foot on his chest. With that, she controlled him, and took Shirish at gunpoint. “Now, no one will break the law,” she declared firmly. “The court will determine the guilty and decide the punishment.”

Shirish sneered. “He will easily escape, and you’ll do nothing.”

“No matter,” she replied, coldly. “I am a servant of the law. I won’t allow anyone to break it. I have sympathy for you, but I cannot allow you to commit a crime.”

“And what if you were in Mini’s place? You’re also a woman,” Shirish taunted.

Kavita paused, her expression hardening. She recalled her painful past. It wasn’t Vijay Singh, it was Rajendra, the man who had ruined her life. The anger she felt towards him swelled within her. This moment wasn’t just about justice, it was personal.

Vijay Pratap Singh tried to take advantage of the situation. He attacked Shirish, but Kavita was prepared. Her instincts kicked in, and she swiftly moved to save

Shirish from the attack. With a powerful kick, she brought him down to the ground.

Kavita threw the knife towards Shirish, saying, "Finish your job. This scoundrel doesn't deserve to be alive."

Shirish stared at her in disbelief, his mind racing with the sudden change in the situation.

"Do it quickly!" she shouted. "My men will be here soon."

She held him at gunpoint as Shirish tied Vijay Pratap Singh's hands and legs again. He then began to finish what he had started, cutting the man's prominent veins.

"Run that way!" she pointed at a different direction.

"I don't want to run. I've finished what I came here to do," Shirish replied.

"I'm allowing you to run. Why don't you want to?" she asked anxiously.

"Madam, if I run, the case won't be closed. I don't want to bring up her name again. She deserves to rest in peace wherever she is. She sacrificed her life for this," Shirish said, his voice heavy with emotion.

"But if I arrest you, the lawyers will dig up all the buried names during the trial," she said, her voice tinged with concern.

"Madam, I'm not asking you to arrest me," Shirish said quietly.

"You mean... No! I can't let that happen," she hesitated, struggling with her emotions.

Shirish smiled faintly. “Madam, Mini sacrificed her life to bury the truth and protect others. If I stay alive and face trial, her name will be dragged through the mud. Her sacrifice will be ruined. I cannot let that happen.”

There was a deep silence between them before he added, his voice steady and filled with resignation, “Both Mini and I made a mistake, I forced her to trust me, and she did. She paid the price for that trust. Now it’s my turn.”

XIX

September 2023

"She is Dulari. I found her when she was just ten years old, abandoned at a railway station. Her father had left her there because he didn't want another daughter in the family. I felt pity for the poor, weeping, hungry child," Mrs Vijay Pratap said to Kavita Singh.

"All right, but my question is still unanswered," Kavita pressed.

"You must first listen to Dulari's story. I promise you'll find it interesting, and you'll get the answer you're looking for," she replied. "So, I found her at the station, back when I wasn't Mr Vijay Pratap Singh's wife, yet." She smiled mysteriously.

"What do you mean?" Kavita asked, surprised.

"At that time, I was married to an honest engineer. But honesty has no value for politicians and senior officers. They shuffled him from one department to another, from one city to the next. Someone advised him to meet Mr Vijay Pratap Singh to solve his career troubles. Whether his problems were solved or not, no one knows, but he did lose his wife." She laughed bitterly, wiping away tears quickly.

She signalled to Dulari, who quietly left for downstairs. Kavita noticed it but said nothing.

Mrs Vijay Pratap continued, "There was another hurdle back then, Vijay Pratap's first wife. One day, while shopping in the market, she was attacked. Vijay Pratap, who was then the state's home minister, ordered the police to catch the attackers at any cost.

"Then, one night, that woman came to me, begging for protection. She claimed Vijay Pratap was desperate to marry me and couldn't wait for a divorce. She had no safe place to go. I believed her fear was real. So, I secretly sent her to my native village, hidden away from Vijay Pratap's reach. She stayed there, in hiding, for over six years."

At that moment, Dulari returned, bringing with her a dignified middle-aged woman dressed in a graceful saree. Mrs Vijay Pratap smiled warmly and offered her a chair.

"She is Madhu Devi, the ex-wife of Mr Vijay Pratap Singh," she said, casually dropping a bombshell that left Kavita stunned.

"She has come to perform Vijay Pratap ji's last rites. After all, he was once her husband too," she added.

"I would appreciate it if you could help in the kitchen and assist the priest. I don't know much about conducting rituals," she said, giving Kavita a polite excuse, though it was clear she wanted to introduce Madhu Devi.

"Oh, of course. I'll manage everything. Please come soon, you must sit with me during the final rituals.

After all, we were both his wives," Madhu Devi said with a gentle smile and went downstairs.

"So, what now? Are you going to share the property with her?" Kavita asked sharply.

"This property is already hers. I simply manage it now, and I intend to contest the upcoming elections by carrying forward the legacy of this royal family," she answered confidently.

"It's a nice story, but how does it answer my question?" Kavita asked again, still unconvinced.

"I haven't finished yet. I promise you'll have your answer once I'm done," she said with a small smile.

She continued, "After I hid Madhu Devi in my village, the path was clear for Vijay Pratap to marry me. He didn't bother searching for his missing wife. In a simple ceremony, he married me. I came to this house with my so-called daughter, Dulari. We lived happily for over five years... until the day I saw him in a compromising situation with someone."

"Wow! So, Mr Vijay Pratap found yet another woman to satisfy his endless lust. Now I see why you did all this; you were afraid he would do to you what he did to his first wife," Kavita said, a little too eagerly.

"I see how quickly you jump to conclusions," Mrs Vijay Pratap said dryly. "But I still haven't finished my story."

"You mean to say my conclusion is wrong?"

"Who am I to stop you from drawing conclusions? But please do me a small favour, let me finish the story first," she said with a sardonic smile.

"So, what's left to tell?" Kavita asked, impatient now.

“Don’t you want to know who the woman was, the one I caught with my husband?” Mrs Vijay Pratap said, her voice taking on a bitter tone.

“Who was she?” Kavita asked, Mrs Vijay Pratap’s tone making her deeply curious.

“She was my foster daughter, Dulari,” she replied, her voice trembling. “He had been assaulting her since she was only thirteen. He scarred her body, shattered her soul, and broke her spirit. The silence I had once mistaken for respect... was actually fear. I wanted to protect Dulari from every hardship, but I had never realised there was a monster living under my own roof. I couldn’t save her. I failed her.”

Tears streamed down her face as she began to weep bitterly. Holding Dulari’s shoulder, she cried out, “Please forgive me, Dulari! I couldn’t save you!”

Kavita Singh stood in stunned silence, at a loss for words. All she could do was watch them cry. Quietly, she picked up a glass of water and handed it to Mrs Vijay Pratap, gently patting her back to comfort.

When she had calmed down a little, Mrs Vijay Pratap continued, “Every day, many people came to meet my husband. One day, Shirish arrived in the disguise of a farmer. But he didn’t ask for help or explain any problems. Instead, he slipped inside and started asking his PA about my husband’s routine. I found this behaviour suspicious, so I kept an eye on him.”

She paused briefly before continuing. “Around the same time, you came to warn my husband about the murder threat. You didn’t notice, but Shirish was standing right behind you. He heard everything, your information, your warning. After you left, I confronted him, pretending I had caught him red-handed.

He panicked and tried to run. That confirmed my suspicions. I let him go on one condition: he would meet me at DLF Mall that evening.

"That evening, I learnt the ugliest truth about my husband. I had already decided to kill him. Shirish only gave me one more reason to justify my decision. I gave him all the information he needed. Together, we made a plan. I sent a message to Sabala's husband from an unknown number, pretending to be my husband's PA. A woman was the easiest bait for Vijay Pratap. Shirish then messaged him, pretending to be the agent of a famous model in need of help. My husband could never resist helping a woman, especially a beautiful one. He called Shirish to his farmhouse... and the rest, you already know."

Silence fell between them. Each waited for the other to speak. At last, Mrs Vijay Pratap broke it.

"I chose to help Shirish because there was no legal way to punish my husband for his crimes. Had he lived, he would have ruined many more lives. I believe that's the same reason you allowed Shirish to go through with it. In that sense, you and I are sailing in the same boat. I don't feel guilty for what I did, and I don't think you should either. That's why I publicly thanked the police for their tireless efforts, so that no one would suspect you or question your role in all this. If you still find me guilty, you're free to arrest me."

Kavita finally spoke, "Why would I arrest you? The murderer of the great Vijay Pratap Singh is already dead, killed in a police encounter. I've come here only to thank you for supporting us during such a difficult time. Please accept my deepest condolences for the untimely death of your husband."

Mrs Vijay Pratap offered a faint, sorrowful smile. “May I ask you something?”

“Of course. It would be my privilege to honour your request,” Kavita replied.

“I know you’re working to save Chatar Singh from capital punishment. It’s my humble request, please don’t reveal the dark truth about my husband while doing so. Let it be buried with him.” She folded her hands in a silent plea.

“You have my word,” Kavita said firmly.

“Please join us for his last rites,” Mrs Vijay Pratap invited.

EPILOGUE

2024

The court hall was quieter now, but beneath that silence pulsed the echo of long suppressed truths. After years of manipulated facts and silenced voices, the Sabala case file had been reopened not with noise, but with clarity. The police filed a revised charge sheet naming Vijay, Nitin, Ajay, and Rahul as the main accused. It was a quiet admission that the system had failed, deliberately, devastatingly.

The charge sheet dismantled the original investigation led by Inspector Devendra Kumar, revealing how fake evidence, coerced witnesses, and falsified reports had conspired to bury the truth. The very machinery meant to protect justice had been used to strangle it.

What shook the court most was not just the corruption. It was how the truth had resurfaced.

The charge sheet revealed that Shirish, Sabala's childhood neighbour, had learnt the truth from a constable posted at the same station during the investigation. Under the influence of alcohol, the constable let slip what should have never been hidden. That one careless confession became the turning point.

Outraged by the injustice done to Sabala, Shirish was provoked to take matters into his own hands. He operated outside the law—alone, unheard, and unacknowledged—yet his efforts forced the truth to the surface.

Shirish believed it was Vijay Pratap Singh who had corrupted the case. But, as the revised charge sheet revealed, the truth was more grotesque: Ajay, Vijay Pratap's nephew, had used his uncle's name to shield himself and twist the entire investigation. Power was used not just to protect a criminal, but to erase a victim.

The court, shamed by the truth, withdrew the death sentence earlier imposed on Chatar Singh. His innocence had been crushed beneath false testimony and bureaucratic convenience. Now, after years of darkness, the gates of justice finally creaked open for him.

Inspector Kavita Singh stood quietly at the back of the courtroom, and so did Mrs Vijay Pratap, two women who had walked the tightrope between truth and consequence. They had made their choices, and in the end, those choices helped tilt the scales towards justice.

Shirish's name was not mentioned in the courtroom. His photo was not printed in the papers. There would be no medals or memorials for him.

But none of this would have happened without him.

He was the crack in the wall that had let the light in; the ghost who would never be seen, but whose fingerprints were on every truth that came out.

Justice did not roar in this case. It arrived slowly: quiet, bloodstained, and long overdue.

But it came.

ABOUT THE AUTHOR

Ashish Sharma is a novelist and scriptwriter known for his gripping crime thrillers, mysterious dramas, and emotionally resonant romances. With a background in science and biology, Ashish brings a sharp, analytical eye to his stories, weaving in medical and forensic details that add depth and authenticity to his work.

Currently working as a sales professional in a pharmaceutical company, Ashish regularly interacts with people from diverse backgrounds, cultures, and walks of life. This exposure fuels his storytelling with real-world struggles, folklore, and untold stories often hidden from the mainstream narrative. His ability to observe human behaviour, empathise with different perspectives, and uncover emotional truths, gives his writing a rare and relatable intensity.

A passionate reader and music enthusiast, Ashish finds inspiration in everyday conversations and the nuanced experiences of those around him. He has already authored four novels and continues to explore bold and intriguing themes in his upcoming projects.

Ashish lives in Delhi with his life partner and two children.
